Up at the 'Sky Edge' 1917

Mark J Foster

Contents

Introduction.

Chapter 1 - **The Raid.**

Chapter 2 - **William George Francis.**

Chapter 3 - **Samuel Garvin.**

Chapter 4 - **West Riding Regiment.**

Chapter 5 - **A.W.O.L.**

Chapter 6 - **Return to Sheffield.**

Chapter 7 - **Return to France.**

Chapter 8 - **Sheffield or Bust.**

Introduction.

Samuel Garvin and George Mooney, were both illustrious individual's, and being much characterised by local folklore, during the earlier part of the twentieth century with regard to history of the city of Sheffield. Both were leaders of the opposing fractions of the 'Mooney and Park Brigade' razor gangs, as their conflict would escalate into the brutal episode of the 'Sheffield Gang Wars,' in the aftermath of World War One.

Their prize, for control of the lucrative 'Sky Edge' gambling ring, situated at a secluded site high above the city. Providing an ideal vantage point, to which many willing 'punters' were able to participate, in all forms of illegal gambling activity.

Sheffield was a rapidly expanding industrial city of the time, and had concentrated on the manufacture of Steel and other associated Engineering products. The city had grown rapidly during the earlier years of the 'Industrial Revolution' and attracted workers from all parts of the country for work in the mechanised Steel Mills, Forges and Foundries. Yet for so many of the city's inhabitants, having to endure the hardship, poverty, overcrowding and squalor of the rapidly expanding city during the turn of the twentieth century. Illegal gambling, along with alcohol, was often an outlet of escapism for the many working men of the city, with the added possibility to supplementing their meagre earnings. Illegal gambling was much frowned upon by the authorities, and like other such moral and social dilemmas of the time, was soon to be driven 'underground,' and into the control of several unscrupulous, and questionable individuals.

The gambling ring of 'Sky Edge' had its origin during the later years of the nineteenth century, where working men would often congregate after their work shift. Gambling activity increased significantly after 1914, due to the emergence of more available money within the city, as a direct attribute to the upturn of Sheffield's economy, during the 'boom years' of manufacture for the First World War effort.

The book 'Up at the Sky Edge - 1917' highlights the fortunes of two men, who were heavily involved in the early years of the gang struggle. Both were determined to escape from the horror and carnage of the 'Western Front,' and of their return to Sheffield, with the view of control of the 'Sky Edge' gambling ring, during the lucrative war years.

Samuel Garvin was a petty criminal, long before the time of his Army service, as he was soon to take the leading role in the emergence of the 'Park Brigade,' and along with his close associate William Francis, who would be instrumental as a trusted and valued aid, in his struggle to oust the 'Mooney Gang' from 'Sky Edge.'

Sheffield was renowned to be such a violent place at the time, and with both groups emerging from the tough working class areas of the 'Park' district located within the shadow of Sky Edge, and the notorious 'West Bar' area, home to many of the migrant Irish community residing in Sheffield. As the conflict between both groups quickly escalated during the time of the 'First World War' and of the intermediate years following. It would not be until the mid-1920s that the gangs were eventually brought under control, by the questionable policing tactics of Chief Inspector Percy Stiletto, of the Sheffield City Police, and his notorious 'Flying Squad.'

Chapter 1 - The Raid.

Two heavily laden 'Sheffield City Transport Department' Omnibuses slowly climbed the steep incline of Granville Road, as they headed toward the direction of Norfolk Park. As they slowly neared the top of the steep hill, and much to the relief of both the driver and of the struggling Omnibus engines. Both vehicles then turned a sharp left and onto the level surface of Stafford Road, directly opposite the ornate entrance gates of Norfolk Park. Once both Omnibuses had turned onto the level surface of Stafford Road, their engines soon returned back to their normal operating condition, as they continued along the uneven cobbled surface of Stafford Road, located in the upper Park district of Sheffield.

Daylight was now beginning to slowly fade, as the onset of night approached, the gas lit street lamps of Stafford Road, reflecting brightly against the wet cobbles of the road surface. Both Omnibuses had all windows of the lower decks totally obscured by black canvas, and with the exception of the driver. Both highlighted no visible sign of any passengers seated on either the lower or the open upper deck, as they continued their journey along the quiet of Stafford Road. They passed by many of the grand stone built houses that lined this part of Stafford Road, and this being so different to the much poorer housing stock of the lower Park district, that was located less than a quarter of a mile away.

Both Omnibuses began to slow as they now reached their destination, and turned an immediate left into Talbot Place, and through the open large iron gates, into the grounds of the Shrewsbury Hospital. Once both Omnibuses were beyond the gates, the gates were quickly closed by the Hospital Caretaker behind them as they drew to a halt, directly outside of the

Hospital Chapel building. The engines were quickly silenced, as two columns of Soldiers quickly emerged from each stationary Omnibus, as they hastily moved toward a small entrance door of the Chapel building. The Soldiers made their way inside the Chapel building, each man carrying a backpack and rifle, as they hastily made their way inside. Following the haste disembarkation of the Soldiers, the Hospital Caretaker re-opened the Hospital gates, as both empty Omnibuses quickly restarted their engines, and hastily made their way back through the entrance gates and re-commenced with their journey, both now heading toward the city centre.

Although it was now dark outside, no lamps were allowed to be lit within the Chapel, so as to avoid arousing further suspicion as to the Soldiers presence inside the building, that night and of the avoidance of light being further illuminated through the large stained glass window of the Chapel building. Nothing further was seen of the Soldiers that night as they remained silently inside the Chapel building.

The covert operation had begun some two hours earlier, when both Omnibuses had arrived at the Redmires Army camp, situated high on the moors above the western fringes of the city. The lower deck passenger windows of both vehicles, had been 'blacked out,' and were covered over by a dark canvass type material, with the typical 'not in service' sign board being displayed to the front of both vehicles.

Both were standard Sheffield Omnibus vehicles that would be seen in everyday use throughout the city, and were painted in the typical blue and cream livery, of the 'Sheffield Transport Department'. Two groups of fifteen Soldiers had boarded the lower decks of each Omnibus, the operation being overseen by a single Commanding Officer, who had sat inside the lower deck of the front Omnibus. The journey that was being undertaken was certainly secretive, and as to why both vehicles were travelling through the city at such a late hour, was possibly due to fewer townsfolk being around at that time to witness the logistical operation. But in hindsight this was probably not such an unusual sight on the city streets during April 1918, with so much logistical movement of both people and goods, due to the city's crucial role in its support of the 'Great War' effort.

Sheffield had been busy manufacturing for the 'Great War' for the past four years, and was always a hive of activity; transportation and logistics. For the first time in many years, earnings became so plentiful to the men and women employed in the many reserved occupations of Steel and Engineering manufacture. This scenario being so removed to the carnage and often stalemate, currently taking place in the battlefields of Northern France, to which most of the manufactured equipment was destined.

The 'Great War' had seen several of the larger Sheffield manufacturing companies become responsible for the supply of ordnance and other such Military commodities, used during the offensive. Order books were full, as the companies now competed with each other, often offering increased wages to attract the shortage of available labour within the city.

After experiences of the 'Western Front' including the campaigns of the 'Somme, Vimy Ridge' and other such campaigns, many Soldiers were becoming disillusioned by the strategy and progression of the 'Great War.' The stalemate, and pointless suffering being endured by both sides. This being so different from that earlier fervour and enthusiasm being experienced during those earlier days of the war, as was reflected in their patriotic duty toward both 'King and Country'.

Many city Soldiers had returned back to the battlefields of France, following their brief seven day leave periods spent at home, with stories of the money being earned by the men employed in the reserved occupations. To the many city Soldiers serving abroad the stories of the money being earned at home, further added to their homesickness, as the war had reached such a stalemate, and had an unsettling effect upon their morale. Many young men had so enthusiastically enlisted at the beginning of the conflict, and were soon drafted into the newly created 'Pals Battalions,' to serve alongside the regular regiments.

Following recruitment, combat training would be undertaken at Redmires Camp, Edmund Road, and even Bramall Lane during those early months of the war. Initial service postings were to be first spent in Egypt, and after only a few months the 'Sheffield Pals Battalion' were to be drafted into the carnage of Northern France, that was to become known as the 'Somme Offensive of July 1916'. Many of the recruits involved at the Somme had hailed from the 'Pals Battalions,' as they were put to the slaughter by the German guns. The fervour and enthusiasm of those early days, had soon become a distant memory as the realities of war and decimation experienced during the campaign saw many of the newly formed 'Pals Battalions' decimated, and had to be incorporated into the larger regular regiments, following the great losses they had endured.

The Shrewsbury Hospital site was situated in a relative quiet part of the city, on a headland overlooking the city centre, its isolated location being well away from the heavy industry and pollution, which dominated the lower lying areas of the rivers Sheaf and Don valleys below. With the cleaner air, being blown directly from the Derbyshire hills, the location was seen as an ideal site to enable the recuperation of patients residing within the

Hospital. The Hospital and associated Alms houses were both built by the Duke of Norfolk, as a legacy to the philanthropy of the 7th Earl of Shrewsbury, and developed a trust to provide respite and care, to the many poorer, infirm townsfolk. It enabled them to be nursed within relative isolation, and well away from the noise, dirt, and disease of the city below. The centre piece of the Hospital complex was the large stone built Chapel building, towering above the smaller Hospital buildings, an impressive sight that embodied the 'christian value' of both the Earl and Duke, as was an integral part of the daily regime of beneficiaries under the care of the Shrewsbury Hospital.

Aside from the Hospital Caretaker and the General Manager, no one was aware as to whom were inside of the Chapel on that night, such was the secrecy of the planned operation. The Soldiers inside were ordered as to keep their conversation to the minimum in hushed tones, and to remain inside the Chapel building at all times. As the night progressed, a small gas lamp was allowed to be lit by the Commanding Officer and this was ordered to being dimmed to a minimum, so as not to highlight any activity inside, during the early hours. It was now mid-April, and was still cold in the night air outside of the Chapel building. Although most of the Soldiers stationed inside the Chapel building, had previously been billeted at the Redrmires camp throughout the past winter months. So the night spent inside the Chapel building would be quite a luxury, in comparison to the wooden huts and tents, to which they slept whilst at the Redmires camp, situated on the edge of the bleak Hallam Moors.

The Soldiers were quietly awakened at around four o clock on the following morning, as each was given the part of a small loaf, and a cut of butter placed within their ration can. The Commanding Officer then briefed the men as to their objectives of the days undertaking. At four thirty, the order was given to vacate the Chapel, as all backpacks were to be left inside the building, and each man was issued with a ten foot length of rope which was to be wrapped around and hung over their left shoulder. Bayonets were ordered only to be fixed, when at the arranged rendezvous point, so each man was to carry his rifle unlatched whilst moving. The Commanding Officer then highlighted on a map the designated route and highlighted a redevouz point as to where the Soldiers were all to gather, being the first objective of the operation. He went on to highlight the importance of moving quickly, and the avoidance of any possible detection at this early hour.

The men were to leave the Chapel building in pairs, the Commanding Officer and another Soldier leaving first, and the rest to follow on at one minute intervals. They were to proceed quickly along a designated route of along Talbot Place, crossing over Duke Street and then proceed the short distance along the Manor Oaks Road, to the designated rendezvous point at the notorious 'Sky Edge'. The streets were dark and deserted at this early hour, as each pair of men hastily made their way outside and headed toward the rendezvous point, that was situated on a hillside within a small wooded area, located above the Manor Oaks Road. The Commanding Officer and Soldier left first, and both had great difficulty in keeping their generated noise to the minimum as the clatter of their boots along the stone pavement flag stones reverberated and echoed along the deserted streets. Each man was fully aware of the route to be taken and was to progress at speed to avoid any detection, as they began to leave the Chapel building in pairs at one minute intervals, and out into the cold and darkness of the early morning air.

The rendezvous point was to be at the notorious 'Sky Edge,' a prominent headland located to the east of the city centre, being much favoured for its high prominent position of open heath and woodland high above the city. The site affording an excellent vantage point, as to the look out for potential Police raids, whilst the undertaking illegal gambling activity that took place at the site. During daylight hours, the whole area would be posted with men acting as look outs, as these were known locally as 'Pikeys,' with the Police often foiled in they're undertaking of any raids within the area, and with 'Sky Edge' having numerous escape routes in several directions.

The whole objective of the operation, and the reason for the Soldiers being placed up at the 'Sky Edge' at such an early hour, was to strategically prepare and to secure the whole area, before the many patrons of gambling activity would arrive later that morning. The Soldiers were to be placed at various locations throughout the site, and the rough terrain of the former quarrying activity and woodland, of the area, would ensure they had ample hiding places until the raid was ordered to be commenced. The Soldiers were all here, not as guardians of the peace, or to make arrests for any illegal gambling activity, as that would be the role of the Sheffield City Police. But they were here to find 'Great War' deserters, who would often be known to gravitate toward the gambling rings, and of the prospect of earning some easy money, whilst on the run.

Once at the redevouz point, the Soldiers were divided into smaller groups of three men each, and were directed by the Commanding Officer to take cover at several strategic key locations identified throughout the site. The groups being placed close to known escape routes, as their objective being to surround and apprehend all participants at the site for further identification. The raid was to take place at the sound of a charge whistle, discharged from the Commanding Officer at a designated time later in the morning.

All of the Soldier's involved in the raid on that cold April morning were newly recruited, and this would be their first experience of a 'live charge,' and of the possible use of live ammunition. The single blast of the 'charge whistle' was an order for the men to 'advance,' and would be the very same sound that was to be the last order heard by many of their counterparts whilst serving in France. The city Police were also fully aware of the raid that was taking place on that morning, and had spent the earlier part of the morning, sat waiting in several unmarked vehicles, located near to the entrance of the Nunnery Colliery located toward the opposite end of the Manor Oaks Road.

Following the securing of the Sky Edge site, 'three successive shots' were to be fired into the air, to signal to the waiting Police, that the site could now be accessed. Accompanying the unmarked Police vehicles at Nunnery Colliery, was an Army truck, assumed to be simply collecting coal for the use at Redmires camp. Inside this vehicle were four Military Police Officers, patiently waiting for the signal to advance and that the site, was secure.

At around eight o clock, a small group of men had now began to arrive at the 'Sky Edge' site taking the well-trodden and steep path up toward the site, from Duke Street below. This early group began to sweep away leaves and other such debris, from the bare earth 'pitch and toss' rings, that were intended to be used later that day. Observations by the Commanding Officer in charge of the operation could now clearly identify that there was a single man in this early group, whom appeared to be in charge and could clearly be seen instructing several younger youths with various duties around the site. A confrontation had quickly developed between two of the youths firstly involving pushing and arguing, that soon escalated into a fist fight between the youth. They were quickly surrounded and encouraged by the others, who now all stood watching the confrontation. The fight lasted for around five minutes, before being broken up by another older looking man, who had now arrived up at the site. He quickly pushed both youths into different directions, and had ordered them toward lookout posts at two entrance locations on the site, as he then sat down onto a large rock smoking a cigarette, as several others now began to arrive at the site.

Around nine o clock the whole area had come to life, and this being so different from that earlier calm of the dawn morning, as betting against the game of 'pitch and toss' began for the day. It could be observed by the Commanding Officer that an estimated crowd of around eighty men, had now gathered at the site to participate. Many men were still dressed in their work overalls, and had possibly arrived at the site straight from work following a night shift, whilst others were dressed of a much smarter and cleaner appearance.

At exactly nine fifteen, the Commanding Officer rose up to his feet from the foliage, and blew into his charge whistle, to signal the advance of his men. In the confusion of the advancing Soldiers, money was grabbed from the 'pitch and toss' rings in an attempt to be hidden, as the group desperately tried to move away from the advancing Soldiers. Their exit was soon thwarted by the placement of Soldiers at other key locations throughout the site, and all of the men at the site, were surrounded and apprehended. The Soldiers now with their bayonets attached to their rifles, could not be overwhelmed as all the gathered men stood quietly, now encircled by the Soldiers awaiting their fate. The Commanding Officer then ordered his men to divide the apprehended men into smaller groups of five men each, and instructed each to be individually searched, for the possibility of any weapons being carried. After each search, the group of five men were then tied up together, using the rope being carried by each Soldier, and were ordered to sit onto the ground. Once all of the apprehended men had been searched and tied up, the site was now secure. The Commanding Officer ordered a Soldier to fire 'three successive shots' directly into the air, to signal to both the Sheffield City Police, and the Military Police, that the site was now secure.

After several minutes, the approaching vehicles could clearly be heard travelling along the Manor Oaks Road, as they now headed toward the direction of 'Sky Edge'. Nothing further was said to any of the apprehended men, by either the Commanding Officer or any of his men. Several of the apprehended men now began to hurl verbal abuse toward both the Commanding Officer and the Soldiers watching over them, as the captors watched over the men, tightly clutching their rifles and unfazed by any of the abusive language, or of the pleading of innocence.

A group of eight Police Officer's, and four Military Police Officers, now arrived at the site, as a Police Sergeant now addressed all the apprehended men. They were told, they were all under arrest, for the participation of an illegal gambling activity, within the jurisdiction of the city of Sheffield. A Military Police Officer then stepped forward, and asked for any man currently serving with 'His Majesties Armed Forces,' to make themselves known to him. None of the apprehended men highlighted they were 'absent without due leave,' and all were assumed to be civilians.

The apprehended men remained silent, as the Police Sergeant, instructed his Officers, to individually untie each group in turn, so as to enable each man to be handcuffed and further questioned. Many of the men refused to give their names, or provide other such details of identification to the city Police, as this would be quickly met by a swift response, in the form of a strike from a truncheon, across the upper arm, or of successive blows toward their lower torso. Men still tied up in the other groups were all to witness the punishment being dealt, and had soon subconsciously decided to co-operate, and to reveal their identity to the Police. As each man was questioned, a Military Police Officer stood alongside the interrogating Police Officer, and looked closely at each man. He held a leather satchel, containing various papers and several photographs of service deserters, known to have originated from the Sheffield area.

Several men being individually questioned, were soon recognised from the photographs being carried by the Military Police, including a known member of the 'Sky Edge' hierarchy, a man known as Samuel Garvin who had absconded from France, and deserted from the Army some two months earlier. After questioning he was handcuffed by a Military Police Officer and taken over to another part of the site, where he was then placed under armed guard along with two other apprehended service deserters. Stood directly next to Samuel Garvin, as the men were being questioned was a large and well built man who gave his name as William Francis. He was not identified from any of the photographs or from the papers that were being carried by the Military Police, so he was apprehended to be charged by the city Police, and moved to another part of the site where the majority of the men were being held.

Francis was then ordered along with the other civilian men to follow the arresting Officers and escorted down to the Water Lane Police Station located within the city centre. All to be charged with the participation of illegal gambling activity, and any monies upon their person, being confiscated from them by the Police at Water Lane.

The three men, who had earlier been identified and apprehended as known deserters, were handcuffed by the Military Police, and immediately escorted to the Victoria Railway Station, where they were placed under Military guard, and escorted to the Catterick Garrison in North Yorkshire. The raid was highlighted by both the city Police and the Military Police as a successful undertaking, with three known deserters from the Sheffield area, being apprehended from 'Sky Edge,' on that morning.

At the Water Lane Police Station, the civilian men were then subjected to further rough treatment, in order to obtain their signed confessions, but also to further affirm their correct identity. Around seventy men including William Francis were all crammed into the five small holding cells located in the basement of the Police station, as to await their fate at the hands of the City Magistrates on the following morning. Each man was brought out individually for further questioning by the Duty Sergeant, and again were hit and roughly treat to affirm their correct identity, and other such details the Police were unsure about . William Francis was the next man to be questioned, he was a strong and powerfully built man. Being over six feet tall, he was viewed quite cautiously by the other Police Officers in attendance. He was asked his place, and date of birth?

"Sibsey, Lincolnshire, 6 of September 1897" he replied directly to the question of the Duty Sergeant.

When asked his occupation? he replied as an "unemployed labourer."

This was such a strange occurrence, in a 'boom town' such as Sheffield during this period, and that such an able bodied and strong man could be out of work, when the many Steel and Engineering companies were so desperate for able bodied men.

When he was asked as to why he hadn't been conscripted? his response to the Duty Sergeant was simply "poor eyesight."

The Duty Sergeant was not so convinced with his response, as he then ordered a few more strikes to be directed toward Francis from the sticks and truncheons being carried by the other Officers in attendance. But given both the sheer bulk and strength of Francis, this appeared to have very little effect or discomfort upon him.

Francis gave his current address that he was living in a lodging house, located near to Scotland Street, in the West Bar area of Sheffield. This was a notorious and often troublesome area, occupied by many Irish immigrants who had arrived in the city to find work, and was often to be seen as a 'no-go area,' for the city Police. There was much resentment in the area toward both the Police, and other such representatives of authority, this also being generated by much of the anti-British feeling in the area, at the time.

The Duty Sergeant was quite suspicious with regard to the background information that was being supplied by Francis, and so he requested that another Officer go to further check Francis details against the Military Registration book, that was held upstairs in the Police office. From the information sourced from the Military Registration book, it was highlighted to the Duty Sergeant, that Francis was also identified to be a known deserter, and found to have absconded from the same West Riding Regiment as Samuel Garvin in Northern France, only two months earlier.

The Military Police were alerted by telephone, and the following day Francis was escorted to the Victoria Station, and placed under armed guard by the Military Police to be escorted to the Catterick Garrison North Yorkshire.

Chapter 2 - William Charles Francis.

William Charles Francis was born in the village of Sibsey Northlands, situated deep within the Lincolnshire Fens in September 1897. William was the eldest of three sons born to William senior and Lillian Francis. The area around the village was typically rural, and encompassed the flat, fertile landscape of the fens, so dominated by arable farming The village was situated about eight miles to the north of Boston, and straggled the main Boston to Spilsby Road.

William junior was sent out to work from the age of ten, following the premature death of his father, as he subsequently became the main breadwinner of the family, from such an early age. He had soon developed the reputation as a hard working youth, and being much respected by many of the Agricultural Gang Masters and Farmers within the area, despite his young age. Much of the work he undertook, was typical unmechanised farm labouring, and he was often out in the fields from dawn until dusk. Having to work so hard within his formative years, had contributed much toward the development of his large physique, as he had soon gained such a reputation as a strong and hardworking youth, with an ability to work so relentlessly, often of the same ability of much older men. He was also quite an intelligent youth, given the limited opportunities that were available to him and of his limited schooling, but unlike many other residents of the village at the time, William was able to read and write.

Agricultural work in the Sibsey area, was casual by its seasonal nature, and several Farm Labourers were also employed to help transfer produce onto the small sailing boats, that were used to transport potatoes, corn, and other such commodities to the weekly market held at Boston. William was always chosen to assist with this task, and this would often be the highlight of his working week, during the summer and autumnal months.

Boston was a thriving market town, and linked to the rest of England by the national rail network and sea port, it was the main transport hub for agricultural produce within the area. Boston market was always an opportunity for the local population, from the outlying villages to gather, and William soon became a known regular within the town, and especially around the Wide Bargate area.

Boston was directly linked to the Sibsey area by both the Spilsby Road, and the nearby Stonebridge Drain. The Drain enabled the transport of produce cheaply and directly to the market place, situated in the centre of town. The small boats as used by the Farmers were unloaded at the jetty that was situated alongside the Horncastle Road. Once William had unloaded the produce, and up the steep stone steps onto the market carts, he was pretty much free for the remainder of the day, or until the Farmer might require his services, later in the day. If this was not required, he would often walk the eight miles back to Sibsey Northlands from Boston.

As he grew older he began to frequent the many crowded market day pubs of Boston, and would encounter several individuals with rather questionable and often criminal reputations. With large quantities of money being exchanged within the town on a typical market day, activity involving both illegal gambling and of deception, was often commonplace. Many Farmers and townsfolk, much the worse for drink, were often targeted by these unscrupulous individuals, operating within the town.

Away from the large crowds and bustle of the market place that was located in the Wide Bargate, was a small patch of waste land that was located toward the rear of the New England Hotel. It was here that many illegal prize-fights were held on a typical market day, and William was soon encouraged to participate in such fights against other local farm hands, with large wagers often being placed on the outcome. Francis was usually paid the princely sum of three shillings in his undertaking for a win, and nothing for a loss. But with his youthful speed, bulk, and strength, he had soon developed a reputation for himself in these fights, all undertaken illegal, bare knuckled, and being 'no holds barred' affairs. Soon fighters from other areas of Lincolnshire and beyond, were being brought over to Boston on a market day to face William, often with large quantities of money changing hands.

The meagre amount earned by William for a win, would go to further supplement the family income, and William knew that he was being 'used' by these individuals for their own gain, but he also realised that if he didn't take part, there would always be another youth willing to take his place, and to take the three shillings.

William was now seventeen years old, and the family income was further boosted by his younger brother Arthur working alongside him, he had also managed to negotiate an additional sixpence for his part in the prize fights, such was the reputation he had developed. It was October 1915, and the 'Great War' with Germany, had now descended into the stalemate that was to become the 'Western Front' in Northern France. The weekly market at Boston had now taken on a whole new dimension, with so much of the produce and animals purchased, commandeered directly by the Military. Uniformed Soldiers and Officers were now a common sight in Wide Bargate, on a typical market day.

One particular market day William had noticed the sight and sound of an Army marching band, moving from the 'Central Park' bandstand, as they marched along the Straight Bargate to play in the Town Square outside of the St Bartholomew's church. They were playing many popular tunes of the time, and this added to the whole occasion, as crowds soon lined the route of the band clapping, dancing and singing along, to the popular tunes being played.

The band were in the town as part of a recruitment drive of young men from Boston, with the view to enlist and to join the 'Great War' effort. The recruitment session was being held inside the Boston Guildhall. Several young men had lined the route between Straight Bargate and the Town Square, as young girls were encouraged to pass white feathers to the young men in attendance, and seen to be of recruitment age. The white feather symbolising cowardice, and often used to humiliate young men of recruitment age.

As William watched the band pass by, he was passed a white feather into his hand by a young girl following the band, and was quite taken aback by this gesture. He threw the white feather to the ground , as he quickly moved away from the crowds, and headed toward the 'Little Peacock' public house, located on the narrow street of Wormgate, well away from the noise of the 'pomp and ceremony' that was taking place in the Town Square. He was due to participate in a prize fight later that afternoon at three o clock. But the white feather gesture had deeply troubled him, and had upset his usual 'happy go lucky' nature. He now began to feel a sense of guilt and remorse as a result of the gesture, and sub-consciously began to question his own moral duty within this dilemma. He knew very little about the 'Great War,' of its emergence, its significance, or even why it was happening, all he knew was that the Germans, were the evil enemy of the British people.

He attended the prize fight as had been arranged at three o'clock, but he knew in himself, that he was not in the correct frame of mind to undertake this fight. He had drunk much more than was usual for him before a fight, the consequences of trying to put to the back of his immediate thoughts, the 'white feather' incident. As a direct result of his confused state of mind, and of the alcohol he had earlier consumed, he soon lost the fight. He had succumbed quite easily to the ability of his opponent, in less than five minutes, in front of an angry and much disappointed crowd. Many of the usual small time bookmakers present at the fight, had taken several large bets against his opponent, and were so outraged with William at the losses they had incurred, to this unknown opponent.

As the crowd began to disperse and return to the market, a local Farmer known as Edward Fixter then confronted William, and as to how quickly he had lost to the unknown opponent. Fixter had lost a considerable amount of money on the outcome. William already bloodied and bruised from the encounter, was then attacked by Fixter, who up picked up a short length of discarded timber from the site, to use against him. A severe blow was dealt directly to the side of his head from the timber, as Fixter swore and cursed at William. The blow had caught William totally unprepared, as he stumbled over and fell onto the hard ground. He quickly regained his composure, and climbed back up to a standing position, where he quickly overcome Fixter, with a single and powerful blow directly to the side of his face. Fixter now fell backwards and reeling from the blow, he had hit the ground directly behind him. William could see that Fixter had banged his head on the hard ground as a result of the blow, and that he was now unconscious. In his panic he quickly fled the scene as he disappeared into the crowds, thronging the market in nearby Wide Bargate.

In his panic and confusion, his thoughts were still pre-occupied by the 'white feather' incident, but now the confrontation with

Fixter. He contemplated with the possibility of him having killed or severely injured Fixter with the powerful blow he had administered. He proceeded quickly along Wide Bargate and into the Town Square where he stood next to a queue of young men, stood outside the Guildhall and all waiting to enlist. The band were still playing, as several young girls now walked amongst the queue of young men, passing out drinks of ginger beer and small cakes, as they waited in their turn to enter into the Guildhall. William was both bloodied and dirty from the earlier encounter of the fight, as he stood looking directly along the Straight Bargate. He could see amongst the crowd that two Police Officers were walking toward the direction of the Town Square. As they neared he could see that both Officers were assisting an injured and bloodied man, it was Fixter. William was at first, so relieved that Fixter had made a recovery from the head injury, yet they were now obviously looking for his assailant amongst the market day crowds. He asked another man who was stood in the queue, if he could briefly borrow his cap, and pulling the cap tightly over his head, as he turned to face the brick wall of the Guildhall. Both the Police Officers and Fixter, quickly walked past the line, as they hadn't noticed William stood next to the queue. William had briefly noticed that Fixter looked to be bleeding quite heavily from a head wound, so he now assumed that Fixter was being assisted along to the local Infirmary, to have the wound treated.

The men waiting in the queue were slowly moved forward toward the large oak wooden doors of the Guildhall watched and cheered on, by the gathered crowd in the Town Square. It was soon to be William who had now reached the large oak doors, he pondered as to enter the Guildhall, or the opportunity to simply walk away, and to return home. The earlier 'white feather' incident, had deeply affected his conscience, as he continually relayed the event in his thoughts. In this confused and agitated state, of mind he realised that this was the right thing for him to do. Upon entering through the doors of the Guildhall, his eyes had to quickly re-adjust to the poor light, so different from the brightness of the daylight outside. A Recruiting Officer quickly approached William and asked him to remove his shirt and jacket, and these were placed over an adjacent chair. His shirt was already dirty and splattered with blood from the earlier fight, he was conscious of this, as this was placed under his jacket, and out of the sight of the Recruiting Officer His upper body was also covered in bruises and several abrasions, and he was never questioned about this, by any of the Medical staff in attendance. He was then ushered through to a small side room, to be asked a series of questions by an Army Doctor, and his body thoroughly examined, including the removal of all of his clothing. The Army Doctor being satisfied that he was fit enough undertake active service, then asked him to sign a medical consent form, and once redressed he was ushered him back outside of the room, and into the main hall of the Guildhall. The main hall was a hive of activity, with several queues of young men and Army personal trying to keep some form of order. He was directed to join another queue, at the end of which were sat three Recruitment Officers, two of which were busy using typewriters. As he reached the front of this queue, he was asked to take a seat, and was asked several questions with regard to his occupation, family details, as several forms were to be completed by the interviewing Officer, and passed over to the typists who were sat immediately behind him.

He was then asked to stand, and to place his hand on a bible. He was asked to turn to face toward a portrait of the King that had been placed on a wooden stand directly to the left of the desk and to swear his allegiance to the King, by reading from a pre-written card, which was held in front of him. He was then asked to sign the 'Recruitment Undertaking,' and this being the point where civilian men, would now sign to be willing to lay down their lives, for the 'Great War' and of their allegiance to both the King and their country.

This would be the defining moment where William could simply exit the Guildhall, and walk back home the eight miles to Sibsey Northlands, and in the hope that he might be excused future Military service, and to possibly occupy a reserved occupation within the 'agricultural war effort.' But the thought of all this excitement, and of the opportunity to travel away from Sibsey Northlands, was now at the forefront of his thoughts.

Without any hesitation William quickly signed the form, and with no further thought, or consequence of his action.

He was given a 'shilling,' and then passed a green sash to wear over his jacket. William Charles Francis was now an enlisted recruit of the Lincolnshire Regiment he felt so proud of his undertaking. He was then passed a typed piece of paper which highlighted his recruitment number, which would later transcribe to become his Army role number, and also printed on the paper, was a date due in one month's time, where he was to attend back at the Guildhall, to undertake his basic Army training. As he made his way back outside the Guildhall and into the crowded Town Square, the band were still playing, as a young girl walked up to him, and on this occasion passed him a flower with a kiss to his cheek. He then headed toward the Brown Cow Inn on Wide Bargate, as he entered into the bar he was greeted with a loud cheer, and he was soon feeling merry from the endless supply of free drinks, that were being bought for him. Much the worse for drink, a Farmer from nearby Stickford, offered him a lift back home to Sibsey Northlands, on the back of his truck.

Following his basic training William Charles Francis was to be drafted into the 4th Battalion of the Lincolnshire Regiment. His biggest fear now was having to relay this news to his mother. His younger brother Arthur was now supplementing the family income, and his Army pay of one shilling and sixpence per day would also help to support the family whilst he was away. He reached the small family home in a drunken state, his mother relieved that he was home, but so shocked to see the green sash over his jacket, and the recruitment letter, that he passed to her, before he collapsing onto a chair, and descending into a drunken slumber. Naturally his mother was upset at the knowledge of her eldest son now to be leaving home, and it being under such circumstances. The thought of him possibly never returning to the family home, or being severely harmed continually occupied her thought over the following days. The isolation of the 'Fens', and of the Sibsey Northlands community of the time, was that the whole concept of the 'Great War' could have well been over a million miles away, from their thoughts and did not impact upon their everyday lives. Yet here was her eldest son, who had now enlisted, and about to leave home in under a months' time for the first time in his life, to fight against Germany for reasons she knew nothing of. In her mixed emotion she felt so proud of him and only wished her late husband was there to see, but yet she was so sad as to what fate he would encounter and breakup of her close family.

During the month, before his departure to the Army, William was treated as a local hero by the people of the village, he didn't have to buy a single drink in any of the village pubs, and the local store often added many provisions to the Francis family free of any charge, in appreciation of William's enlistment. William began to appreciate that he had done the right thing by enlisting, and that this would be his proud duty to undertake. For the first time in his short life, he now felt that he had achieved something to which him and his family were so proud of, and he only wished that his late father would have been able to witness this.

Before his departure both William and Arthur were offered additional work at several farms within the area, as this would help to supplement the family income further, before William was to leave. This being quite an exceptional occurrence in the area following the harvest, as most agricultural labouring work became so scarce, with many of the Farmers and Gang Masters, able to choose only the best Labourers and to offer much reduced rates, due to the scarcity of the work.

The colder days of November soon arrived, and the day came for William to leave his home and to attend for his basic Army training with the 4th Battalion. The whole family walked together for the quarter of a mile length of Northlands Lane with William. They headed toward the junction of the Boston Road, and to await for the regular Omnibus service that would take William into Boston. Most of the village residents had turned out, and lined the road to bid him farewell, and to offer him their best wishes. There were several gifts of cakes, socks, cigarettes, and apples, for his journey, as he passed villager residents waiting to greet him outside of their homes. The local children and their School Master, had all gathered outside the School House, and sang the hymn 'All things Bright and Beautiful' to him as he passed them by. He had never felt as proud in his whole life before, and now he couldn't wait until the day he would be able to return, and dressed in his Army uniform. As the family made their way toward the triangular shaped wooden shelter, situated at the junction of the Boston Road, they all stood and waited nervously in silence for the Omnibus to arrive.

The engine noise from the Omnibus could be heard slowly approaching from the direction of the village of Stickney, as William took a long fleeting glance across the lonely flat Fenland landscape. The Omnibus now slowly came into view, as his mother now hugged her son, and his two brothers tightly shook his hand in turn. The Omnibus drew to a halt at the wooden shelter as William then quickly climbed aboard the bus, and chose not to look at his family or to show his emotion at this sad farewell. He looked straight ahead as the driver engaged gear, and the Omnibus then slowly moved forward toward the direction of Boston.

All enlisted men were due to report to the Boston Guildhall, by twelve noon on that day, as the Omnibus Conductor approached William and asked for his fare. He produced his enlistment letter to which the Conductor then shook him by his hand, and pointed toward three other young men, who were also sat toward the front of the Omnibus, and were also heading for the Guildhall. Francis moved over to the seat behind them, and introduced himself. There he met Charlie Brooks from Spilsby, Frederick Pass from Mareham Le Fen, and Harold Green from New Bolingbroke. All were in their late teens, and like William each looked barely old enough to enlist. All three were also Agricultural Labourers, as their enlistment had coincided with the downturn in work, following the recent harvest. Harold Green had actually seen William before and had watched him fight in Boston on a market day, and admitted to him that he had once won five shillings on to the outcome of his win. The Omnibus made one last stop before reaching Boston, and stopped directly outside St Margarets Church at Sibsey village, here another young man also climbed aboard and produced his letter to the Conductor, as he was also directed by the Conductor, to the group of young men sat near to the front.

Soon all five were men in conversation as to their backgrounds, and what they all envisaged would be involved in their basic Army training. Around thirty minutes later the Omnibus was driving along Straight Bargate and into the Town Square, as it came to a halt directly opposite the Boston Guildhall. It was now eleven fifteen, and many other young men could be seen, carrying bags and cases, and sat around all waiting in all parts the Town Square. William and the other four men alighted from the Omnibus, they all stood outside the building waiting in anticipation for the large double oak doors of the Guildhall to open. Many townsfolk also walked amongst the gathered young men, handing out bags of boiled sweets, socks, and pencils to them.

In what seemed like an age the St Bartholomew's Church bells now came into life, to highlight that it was twelve noon, as soon as the twelfth bell sounded, the inside bolts of the large oak doors could be heard sliding, as both doors now slowly opened. This was now the point, that his life would be changed forever he realised, as he slowly moved toward the large open doors, and into the surreal darkness of the Guildhall beyond them. All the young men then silently and apprehensively moved toward the doors, as nothing could yet be seen inside or beyond the doors, from the brightness of the Town Square, and entered this dark, silent, and uncertain space. Once inside the Guildhall, all of the young men slowly moved forward through the dark entrance foyer, and into the main hall, where here could be seen several men stood in Army uniform. At exactly ten minutes past twelve, the doors of the main hall were closed abruptly behind them and an eerily silence was experienced by the young men. A young looking Army Officer, possibly himself only in his early twenties, stood up on the small stage where he was seated and introduced himself as Captain Bown-Beesley of the 4th Lincolnshire Regiment. He then went on to inform the new recruits, that they were all to be taken by train to the training camp located at Belton Park, near to Grantham. All of the men were then issued with a blue armband, which they were to wear, until their uniform fitting would take place at Belton Park.

Outside of the Guildhall, William could now hear the sound of an assembled Army band that had now began to play, as the recruits were then ordered to line up. A Sergeant wearing a red sash, then stepped forward and instructed the assembled group of recruits, that they were now part of the British Army. As he began to shout several orders in which to form a line, with much of the instruction being totally misunderstood by the new recruits, which had the added effect of making him become even louder in the tone of his anger, in him seeing the haphazard line being formed.

The large doors of the Guildhall were now re-opened, and the group of forty-eight new recruits now lined up by the Sergeant into rows of four men, and instructed to march out of the hall. Outside of the Guildhall, the band were playing, as the recruits began their first attempt at timed marching and so much to the annoyance of the Sergeant, as he ran up and down the line shouting orders in his attempt to speed or slow the men to remain in time. They all made their way toward the Boston Railway Station and were followed the Army band. The short route to the station was now lined with townsfolk, to highlight their appreciation of the young men and as had happened during the earlier recruitment session, several young girls passed the men flowers, as they came forward to kiss several of the marching men. William marching at the end of the row of four, was the recipient of five young ladies who were all keen to kiss him, and was so flattered by the gesture. The band soon reached Boston Railway Station, and the familiar landmark of the large swan statue, located on the top of the Station Hotel, now came into their view, directly adjacent to the railway station.

The recruits marched haphazardly into the station platform, again followed by many of the townsfolk, where a train was already stood and waiting at the platform. The men were now ordered by the Sergeant to halt and to stand to attention. They were then ordered to climb aboard the carriages as the band continued to play on the platform. The engine of the locomotive was now loudly shunting into life. Many of the young men were receiving farewell hugs from families and sweethearts through the open windows of the carriages, whilst William sat looking downward toward the floor of the carriage, and so wanting the train to quickly move away. The sound of the Guards whistle, then drowned out the sound of the band, who then quickly stopped playing, as they hastily climbed aboard the waiting train, William smiled at the effort required to get the bass drum, through the narrow carriage door.

The Guard blew his whistle with two short successive blasts, as the engine slowly shunted into life, as the train jolted and then pulled slowly out of the Boston Railway Station. This was the first time William had travelled on a train, and it was an experience that he had wanted to savour, regardless of all the excitable conversation that was happening all around him. The train now slowly followed the course of the River Witham, and travelling in the direction of Lincoln. A few of the regular Soldiers from the marching band, now wondered along the carriages, in an attempt to make conversation with the recruits, and to highlight many horror stories of what was to happen at the training camp at Belton Park. This had an unsettling effect on some of the men, now clearly worried as to what fate would deliver to them, whilst at Belton Park. William chose to keep his eyes fixed outside of the window onto the River Witham, as he only engaged in conversation with the four men with whom he had earlier met on the Omnibus heading toward Boston. As the train journey progressed, the Fenland landscape soon gave way to gentle rolling hills, that were now appearing toward either side of the River Witham, and once the train was beyond the village of Bardney, the sight of Lincoln Cathedral could be seen towering in the distance.

The train approached toward the outer area of Lincoln, as the giant Engineering works of William Foster and Co now came into view alongside the railway line, William was amazed at the sheer size of this site, and of the flashes and flames that could be seen coming from inside the many giant buildings, as the metal was being worked upon. The train now began to slow down on its approach into Lincoln Railway Station, and came to a sudden halt at the main platform.

Lincoln Railway Station was such a hive of activity in comparison to Boston Railway Station, with both groups of Soldiers and civilians, stood waiting for other connecting trains, to differing parts of the country. The recruits were then directed by the Sergeant toward an adjacent platform, as they all stood and waited for the arrival of a London bound train, en-route from Great Grimsby. It wasn't long before the engine and steam of the London bound train could be seen and heard slowing, as it approached the station platform. The train was already quite full, with many Soldiers and Sailors all in uniform, and all heading toward London. The recruits climbed aboard the already crowded carriages, as William soon realised that these very men, were now possibly on their way to France, and through London toward the Channel ports.

Several of the men were sat singing along inside the carriages, whilst others just like William were in a more sombre mood, obviously concerned in their thoughts, at what fate awaited them. The train quickly pulled away, but had soon drawn to another a halt at Newark Railway Station, where several more Soldiers clambered aboard the London bound train. By now the train, had become quite crowded, and was difficult for the men to move, with many having to stand in the corridors and gangways.

Around twenty minutes later the crowded train came to a halt at Grantham Railway Station, as a call went up from the Sergeant for all of the Boston men to now alight the train, much to catcalls, and cheers from the other men on the train. The Boston men pushed there way toward the carriage doors and through the crowd of men, as their seats were quickly taken, as soon as they stood up, to leave the train. Once on the platform of Grantham Railway Station the men were ordered to line up, whilst the crowded train hastily pulled out of Grantham Railway Station, and continued its onward journey south toward London.

The Sergeant, ordered all of the men to now line up into pairs, as they proceeded to march toward two commandeered agricultural trucks, that were sat waiting for them outside of the station. The men climbed aboard the trucks quickly, as the Sergeant hurried them with his consistent shouting. He was a large well built man possibly in his late forties, and he no doubt took great pleasure in his role of turning these young men, into fighting men. The trucks were both filthy, covered in mud and other debris from their earlier use of that day, as the men held on to each other all stood up, as the trucks negotiated the rutted country lanes, toward Belton Park.

The camp was approached beyond the sentry post by a long narrow and unmade lane, as the trucks bounced roughly about, in the water filled pot holes of the lane. Soon the sound of gunfire could be heard in the distance, as one man in the truck explained that these were the ranges, being used for machine gun training at the camp. Many of the men now broke into smiles of elation at the thought of this prospect, and of the opportunity to fire a live machine gun. Both trucks had soon reached a large grassed area, located toward the centre of the camp and surrounded by several wooden huts on its perimeter, as the men were ordered off the trucks, and ordered to form a line. Three Officers then climbed up onto the rear of a truck, as one Officer undertook a roll call of the men that were stood in the line. Following on from the roll call, the three Officers then stepped down from the truck, and accompanied by the Sergeant walked along the row of the men closely inspecting each man. Each man stood looking directly forward, avoiding any eye contact as the group of Officers and the Sergeant passed them by.

Every third man along the line, was then singled out by the lead Officer, and told to step forward, the Sergeant following the lead Officer then swiftly punched the selected man hard, and directly into his stomach. As each targeted man reeled in the agony at this unexpected blow, any other man who would then assist the injured man were also hit, by a truncheon being carried by another Officer, stood toward the rear of this welcoming party. As the welcoming committee slowly walked along the line, Francis was the next man to be singled out. He was told to step forward, as he was punched directly into his stomach. He was not prepared to accept being hit for no reason, as he then retaliated by hitting the Sergeant with such force, so as to knock him clean off his feet and onto the wet grass. This was not the welcome to the British Army that the recruits had imagined, and within several seconds he was grabbed and being dragged away from the group by four regular Soldiers. He was then thrown into a small windowless wooden hut that was being used as an equipment storeroom, as the door was locked swiftly behind him.

He was left inside the hut for about an hour, as he now noticed it was slowly becoming dark outside, from the feint light being emitted from underneath the locked door. As the daylight outside faded further he could hear voices approaching the hut and of the door being unlocked. Into the hut walked three large and well built Soldiers, who then grabbed him by his clothing, and threw him outside of the door and into the wet mud of the ground outside. One of the men then grabbed Francis from behind, whilst he was punched successively by the other two Soldiers. He was thrown back down to the ground, and kicked until he pleaded with the men for them to stop the beating. At that moment an Officer, and the same Sergeant, with whom he had earlier altercation, now appeared from behind the group. The Officer addressed the muddy and disheveled Francis as he lay on the ground, by stating that he was now the property of the 'Crown,' and he was to do as he was told by his superiors. In his agony he apologised and then nodded in agreement with the Officer, as he received no further beating from the Soldiers, and was taken back to the hut, as the door was locked behind him. The night spent inside the storeroom was a miserable experience, and his first taste of what was to become of Army life. The nighttime temperature dropped and Francis still in his wet civilian clothes, began to feel the cold as he sat against the timber wall of the hut shivering. He was unable to sleep with the intense cold of the night air, and what seemed like an eternity, until the first glimpses of sunlight began to appear under the hut door and birdsong was heard to herald the arrival of dawn. Soon he could hear the voices of several men outside, and clear the sound of a bugle being played to highlight reveille, and the gathering of the men. Much shouting of what could clearly be heard as instructions being given and the frustrated voice of the Sergeant, getting louder with every order relayed.

The lock of the door could be heard turning, as the door slowly creaked open, as he then grimaced at the sudden light that was now bathing the inside of the storeroom. The Officer and Sergeant, were both stood outside of the door. When suddenly the Sergeant, now began shouting at Francis to come outside, and to stand in line with the rest of the men. As the men looked on, Francis was still wearing his mud caked civilian clothes, whilst the other recruits were now stood so smartly, in their new uniforms and boots. The men were all ordered to follow the Sergeant as they were to take part in a five mile brisk route march, on a circuit around the perimeter of the camp. Francis was made to join the recruits, as they were all led by a younger and much fitter regular Soldier. The men attempted to keep in time to the continual 'left, right' order from the lead Soldier. At various points of the circuit, they would be met by the Sergeant, who would simply bark obscenities toward the men. After around ninety minutes the men had returned back toward the centre of the camp, and once more lined up in front of the Sergeant. As he walked along the line of men, he administered a blow directly to each man toward his stomach area. As he approached Francis, two blows in succession were administered toward him, as he then moved swiftly onto the next man. Francis didn't flinch or even react on this occasion, as the other men around him reeled in agony, as the men were excused and to attend the mess hut.

The men entered the mess hut in pain but were all at ease, as Francis was asked by several of the recruits as to what had happened to him, on the previous night as they queued up for porridge. Francis explained his predicament to the others, and was soon tucking into his first meal since his arrival at Belton Park. He barely had the time to finish the porridge and his hot tea, when in walked the Sergeant and immediately ordered Francis up to his feet. He was then instructed to follow the Sergeant outside, as several thoughts crossed his mind, of the possibility of yet another beating that was coming his way. Both men walked briskly in single file, and across a narrow path, that led toward another hut that was situated toward the opposite side of the open space from the mess hut. The door of this hut was opened by the Sergeant, as Francis was then ordered inside.

Once inside it was noticeable to him that this hut was just another storeroom, with a table and a single chair placed into one corner. Francis was then instructed to strip of all his civilian clothes, and to place his clothes onto the single table, as the Sergeant then left the hut. From the other side of the hut walked forward another Soldier, he was wearing a gas mask, as he carried what looked to Francis to be a bicycle pump, as he began to spray him all over with a white powder, being emitted from the pump. Unsure as to what was happening to him, Francis just stood, and was soon covered from head to toe in the white powder. The Soldier made no comment, and then proceeded to spray Francis's dirty civilian clothes, that were laid out onto the table.

Remaining silent, the Soldier walked back toward the far side of the hut, as he removed his mask, and beckoned Francis over toward him. He explained to him that he was now to receive his Army uniform as the other recruits had been issued on the previous day. The Soldier looked him over, as he then walked over to several shelves containing the differing piles of clothing, and carefully selected several items, passing them to over to Francis. He was asked his Army number, which he had previously recited from his recruitment papers, as the Soldier checked the clothing against a list.

From that point onward Francis continued with his basic Army training with no further incidents, in his adaption to Army life. As the weeks passed he was soon to be considered for machine gun training, given both his strength and physical agility. Medical reports deemed his eyesight as being excellent, so his progression to the machine gun corps, was something he was immensely proud of. His training involved the carrying of a collapsed field gun and several bullet belts, over rough terrain for six miles, this was undertaken quite easily, and manageable for a man of his strength.

The training at Belton Park lasted for six weeks, whilst the recruits were slowly converted into fighting men. No leave was granted during this six week period, and at the end of the training only a twelve hour leave period would be granted. This short leave period would make it impossible for Francis to be able to return home to Sibsey Northlands in order to see his family, and then return back to Belton Park within the twelve hours only allotted. Instead, the Boston recruits headed toward Grantham, and to sample their new found if not all too brief, freedom, from Army life. The recruits headed toward the main road from the camp, and had managed to flag down a passing Farmer, and persuade him to give them all a lift into the town on the back of his truck. The Farmer duly obliged, and it wasn't long before they were all stood at the bar inside the Red Lion, and ordering their first taste of beer, in over six weeks.

Several pints later, and the young recruits were soon in a jovial state, as four of the men then decided to visit a 'house of ill repute' situated on the London Road, that they had heard about from the other men back at the camp. Francis was invited to join them, but he politely turned down the offer. He had never been with a woman before, as he then pondered about what would happen if he should die in France, without this experience. But he wanted to meet a girl in a traditional way, and to hopefully get married once the war was over. He had the eye for a particular girl who lived in the village, and worked at the Sibsey Post Office, and she had actually come out to wave him off as he had departed for Boston on the day of his enlistment. He had hoped to ask her out, once the war was over, and he could return home to Sibsey Northlands. He decided to stay with the rest of the group, and enjoy a few more drinks, before their all to brief return back to camp. It was now six o'clock and they were midway through their twelve hour leave period, as the four guys who had earlier visited the 'house of ill repute,'were now back with the rest of the men, and reliving the tales of they're disappointing experiences. The men were by now getting quite hungry, and left the Red Lion to go to a Fish and Chip shop across the main road, to devour some much needed food before continuing further with their mammoth drinking session.

It was soon time to leave and return to camp, as the recruits left the pub singing and undertaking general drunken horseplay, and it wasn't long before a passing Military Police truck had pulled up alongside the men, as they made their way back along the Lincoln Road. "Jump in the back," came the shout from the cab, as a chorus of laughter emerged as several had tried unsuccessfully to negotiate, the rear of the truck, in their drunken state. With some help, they were all stood on the back of the truck, as the Military Police Officer drove onward toward the camp. As they arrived back in camp, and all aware not to disturb either the Sergeant or the other Officers at sleep, as they all tried to keep as quiet as was possible in their drunken state.

As the Military Police Officer pulled away in his truck, and headed back into Grantham to round up more strays, he mentioned to one of the recruits to get a good nights sleep, as they would all be moving out tomorrow. The news travelled quickly amongst the recruits, who were sober enough to take on this news, as soon all had dropped into a beer enhanced sleep once they were all back inside the hut.

At six o'clock on the following morning, the men were all woken and instructed to stand at ease, many still obviously feeling the effects of the previous nights drinking. Into the hut walked an Officer to whom they had never seen before, as he instructed the men to pack all their belongings, and be prepared to move out by ten o'clock later that morning. They were to travel over to France later that day, many men now began to realise as to why they were only granted a twelve hour leave period on the previous day, as they hastily packed their kit bags.

Just like their arrival at Grantham Railway Station those six weeks earlier, the men were stood to attention and were ordered to board a London bound train, to embark on their journey south toward Kings Cross Railway Station in London. The train slowly pulled to a halt at the platform, as the men were ordered to board the train as they jostled through the already crowded carriages The journey to Kings Cross took around two hours, as many of the men remained standing for the entire journey in the crowded carriages. Once they had arrived in London, the Lincolnshire men were transported by Omnibus from Kings Cross over to the Waterloo Railway Station to continue their rail journey to the port at Folkestone, where they would then board a cross channel ferry destined for Calais.

The crossing of the English Channel was rather uneventful to the men, as nightfall coincided with their journey and following their arrival in Calais, the Lincolnshire regiment then learned they were to be posted to the town of Acheux, located within the Picardy region. Once at Acheux they were to be billeted, and involved in logistical duties, in support of the front line.

The men now boarded a waiting train to begin the four hour journey toward Acheux. Upon their arrival it was so noticeable that the weather had turned significantly colder, as snow now began to fall that continued for the next few days adding to the difficulties of the logistical movement, on the already heavily muddied roadways. The men were all quite apprehensive as to where they were to be posted following their brief billeting at Acheax, and soon the inevitable order had arrived that the Lincolnshire's were to relieve the Northern Irish regiment at the front line. Feelings of apprehension and of excitement, were now at the forefront of Francis's conscience, as he contemplated as to what life would be like in the on the front line. It was now the eighteenth of December, so their first experience of the front line would also coincide with Christmas, and this was also to be his first Christmas away from the family home.

The men were sleeping in tents, within a wooded area immediately outside of the town of Acheux, so the continual effort to keep warm in the freezing conditions, was something that now occupied each man. The order had arrived for the men to route march toward the town of Albert, where they would take up positions on the nearby front line. The sound of shell fire, explosions and of automatic weapons became more prominent to the men, as they slowly neared the town of Albert.

During the march, they were continually forced to move over toward the side of the road, and to allow for the passing of Army logistical trucks and Ambulances, as they negotiated the wet mud and snow of the roadway. The men were also made aware of several stray shells and fragments of shrapnel landing near to them, as the strong smell of sulphur and phosphorus lingered within the cold air. Francis was toward the front of the group of men, alongside Charlie Brooks and William Parkin who he had been with, since that first meeting on the Omnibus travelling toward Boston. Men could now be seen heading in the opposite direction to the Lincolnshire men, this was the first batch of the Northern Irish regiment to whom they were to relieve, all were filthy and covered from head to foot in mud.

"You'se all have a nice Christmas out there boys" as one Northern Irishman shouted over to the passing Lincolnshire men.

The Officer at the front of the group had now halted the men, as they were instructed to wait in what were the remnants of a former woodland, now made up of several burned and shattered trees. The Officer quickly disappeared along another trail, which led directly from the roadway, as it was assumed that this trail would link to the rear communication trenches. The Officer then reappeared after around ten minutes, as he told the men to keep low, and to follow him in single file. They proceeded quite hastily along this trail, for approximately two hundred yards, at the end of which, dropped down into a communication trench. The bottom of the trench being a mixture of both mud and standing water, up to around eighteen inches deep in places. The line of men waded through this, and were continually being passed by the men of the Northern Irish regiment passing in the opposite direction. The haphazard and curving formation of the service trenches, made it difficult for the men to comprehend, as to how near they were to the front line, they're only indication being the increase in the depth of the trenches, and of their increased fortification of sand bags and barbed wire, now lining the parapet of the route.

Upon reaching the front line of trenches, the men had noticed several 'fire steps' that were dug from the trench wall, as these were placed every ten or so yards along this trench sector. The 'fire steps' were to each be manned by three men each taking turns to monitor possible German attacks from across the 'no man's land.' The stench seemed horrendous to the men during this first experience, but they would soon became immune to the smell. The noise of both nearby exploding shells, and of the highly pitched screech as they passed overhead the trench, made several men feel very uneasy at the situation. The fear of a possible German attack upon the trench, was something that quickly disturbed any opportunity for a rest, and sub consciously affected each man, as they tried to capture any possible sleep opportunity. Francis, Brooks and Parkin were ordered to man the number seven 'fire step' in the sector. As they all took a turn of two hours watch each, the step was well fortified above the parapet of the trench wall. Several sand bags were constructed along the parapet, and a small opening, that was just wide enough for the rifle to slightly move in either direction, with the sight engaged, to allow for potential sniping opportunities. The Germans realised this, and often counter shots were simply aimed toward the small opening within the sandbags. No further advances from either side were made during these few days, and was possibly due to the area of no man's land being covered by a blanket of snow, and thus making any activity easily identifiable, especially during a potential night time raid.

Aside from the cold and damp of the trench conditions, and with the little shelter being offered, all three men seemed to enjoy the occasional exchange of gun fire with the enemy, to simply relieve the boredom of their inactivity. It would not be long before the true horror of a mechanised war, were to be experienced by the Lincolnshire men. After only three days spent at the front line, all three men were alerted to the blast of several Officers' whistle's which now progressed along the line of the trench. They were all sounding as three short successive blasts, which they knew from training, highlighted a possible gas attack. Brooks along with several other men, then ran along the trench toward the command post situated about fifty yards further along. He was dismayed to find that no gas masks had been issued to the Lincolnshire's, and none were available for any man positioned in that section, as the Northern Ireland regiment had taken their own gas masks out of the trenches with them.

An Officer at the command post advised on the use of soaked urine to the men, with the ammonia being used to counter the effects of the Chlorine gas being released by the Germans. Inside the command post, another Officer was quickly tearing up small sheets from a blanket, into pieces of approximately one foot in diameter, and quickly passing these to the gathered men. A make shift earth privy was situated near to the command post, as one man laid onto the earthy floor of the privy and dipping handfuls of cloths into the urine and other debris contained within the earth toilet. These were hastily passed back along the line to the waiting men. Brooks ran back over to both Francis and Parkin, with three urine soaked cloth's, and instructed them to cover their faces, much to their disgust and bewilderment of this instruction. All three men, then crouched down with the urine soaked cloths now covering their faces. The faint smell of the Chlorine gas had now descended into this sector of the trench, and soon several agonising cries could be heard, coming from further along the sector. As the Chlorine gas slowly crept along the trench, and would react with and burn the exposed skin of any uncovered man.

The Officer, who had earlier advised on the use of urine, had been a Chemist before the war, so it was so fortunate for the men within this sector, that they were quickly advised to undertake this emergency action. Other men were later seen passing through the sector, and several were in such a state of distress, as many were blinded as a result of the gas attack. The gas dispersed as quickly as it had arrived in the trench, as Parkin moved back up toward the 'fire step' as ordered by the Commanding Officer. It was well known that the Germans would often launch an attack, directly following the chaos of a gas attack. Francis sat down at the foot of the step having now washed his face in the dirty water of the trench floor, to rid himself of the putrid smell of urine upon his face from the soaked cloths that had so prevented him from being affected by the gas.

As he sat down below the 'fire step' in his attempt to calm down after the events of the past few minutes, he felt a gentle splatter upon his face. Thinking nothing unusual of this, he gently wiped the splatter from his cheek, as he looked downward toward his hand he could now see that the tiny splatter he had earlier wiped away from his cheek was blood. He looked around and saw nothing unusual so he sat below the 'fire step' trying to catch some precious sleep, before it would be his turn back on the 'fire step.' He was soon wide awake and unable to sleep possibly due to the adrenaline of the recent activity. He searched through his pockets for his packet of cigarettes and then offered Parkin a cigarette from the packet. Parkin didn't respond to Francis's offer of the cigarette, and thinking he had nodded off on the 'fire step,'he tugged onto Parkin's trouser leg, and again was met with no response. Being concerned that Parkin would be placed on a charge if he was caught asleep by an Officer. He attempted to shake his leg, Parkin again unresponsive, then fell backward and tumbled down onto the mud of the trench floor, his rifle engaging through the sandbags as he fell. He was unresponsive, as Francis tried to lift his head out of the mud, and onto his lap with a view to reviving him. Blood now flowed onto Francis's long coat, from a wound he could see on Parkin's head, as it was soon to be discovered that a bullet from a German sniper, had passed directly through his forehead and exited toward the rear of his head. Parkin was dead, as both Brooks and Francis lifted him out of the mud and laid him onto the fire step in a further attempt to revive him. An Officer arrived at the fire step, as he quickly ordered Brooks back up onto the fire step, to maintain the cover of the position. Parkin's rifle was still hanging in the firing slot of the sand bags, as Brooks slowly removed this, so as not to attract further attention from the German sniper. Brooks was now apprehensive about being in this position on the 'fire step' knowing that a bullet could penetrate these defences at any second, as he prayed quietly to himself, in an attempt to avoid a similar scenario to Parkin.

The Officer and Francis then carried the body of Parkin toward a communication trench, where they simply laid him down onto the mud of the trench floor, at the side of another dead man both awaiting collection from the stretcher bearers. Francis was still in a state of such shock, as he took one last look at Parkin, as he thought back to that early November morning where they had both met on the Omnibus, during their journey into Boston.

Francis returned to join Brooks, who was still nervously stood on the fire step, and he could be seen physically shaking in his anticipation of being hit by the sniper. Francis asked him if he wanted to be relieved, but Brooks insisted he continue until the end of his watch. Things quietened down the over the following few days, as the men began to think of Christmas and of life back at home, and replicated by their German counterparts.

December the twenty-fourth arrived, and as darkness descended on this special night, as the men in the trench were quite surprised to hear raised voices and the singing of carols, coming from the direction of the German trench. This quickly descended into an unofficial carol singing competition, emerging from both sides of 'no mans land,' as this was to highlight the human face of the war. The Germans favourite carol seemed to be 'Silent Night,' which was sung several times during the night, to the words of 'Stille Nacht'.

No further shelling or shooting was committed by either side during Christmas Eve, as most men were able to get some much needed rest. At daybreak on Christmas morning, the weather was cold but being bright and dry. As Charlie Brooks had stood up onto the 'fire step,' and alerted the other men, to red cross flags that were being waved by the German's. Several German Soldiers now began to appear above the parapet of their trench. The British sector all held their fire, and this was seen as an opportunity for both armies to collect their dead, or to search for any surviving injured from 'no mans land.' Soon several British Soldiers were also seen above the parapet further along the sector, as both armies nervously moved toward each other. The first groups of Soldiers to meet simply shook hands, and very soon both Francis and Brooks were walking toward the German front line, as they looked upon the scene of utter destruction within 'no mans land.' They were greeted with the comment of "Es macht mir Kummer" from several German Soldiers stood within the area, and they were unsure as to the translation ('it causes me such sorrow'), as they later learned.

Bodies were being recovered by both sides, and taken toward the rear of the opposing trench systems, one British Soldier had actually slipped and fell into a large water filled shell hole, as he suddenly reappeared being helped back out by German counterparts, as both groups of men stood laughing together at his mishap. Within minutes of this happening, a shell had exploded high above them, fired by the British position further back from the trench system, it was now obvious that some high ranking Officer was not happy with this fraternisation of the enemy. The Soldiers then turned and ran back toward their respective trenches and the all too brief encounter with the enemy was quickly over, and it was so respectful that no further exchanges of fire were administered from either side, on that particular Christmas Day.

Both Francis and Brooks manned the fire step watch, as a pair for the following two days, until they were allocated another recruit to replace Parkin on their watch. The man was called Fred Arnold, who hailed from the village of Clarborough near to Retford in Nottinghamshire. All three men seemed to get along considering the circumstances into which they were all placed. As the New Year of 1916 arrived, at the stroke of midnight on New Year's Eve the Germans launched a series of sixteen improvised flares, that all exploded upon their descent toward the ground. Brooks questioned as to why the British Officers were not as informal, or as easy going as the German Officers seemed to be, and to allow for this type of celebration in the middle of a war zone.

Toward the middle of January word had soon spread around the trench, that the Lincolnshire regiment were to be relieved in two days time, and were to be given a period of recuperation. Francis's first experience of trench life, aside from the death of Parkin, had been quite an uneventful experience. Within two days, the roles were reversed as the muddied and disheveled Lincolnshire regiment now left the trenches, to be replaced by the Northern Ireland regiment.

They wearily walked back toward the town of Albert, and in replication of the sight that greeted them of the Northern Ireland regiment back in December, they were now all filthy and caked in mud. The weather was cold and frosty as the men were still unable to get warm, even due to the long march to Albert. As they reached Albert, they were directed inside what looked to be a former factory unit, now being commandeered by the Army, and were each given a hot meal of bacon and eggs, followed by several cups of hot tea, within the large mess hall. Many of the men soon began to feel tired both due to the warmth of the mess and of eating so well after the previous rations of the front line. Upstairs in a large room within the factory building were several rows of galvanised bathtubs, which were all being filled with hot water from a large copper tank on wheels, as it progressed down the row of bathtubs. Francis was ordered to follow Brooks after his bath, as the same water had to be used for up to four men. The second, third and fourth man were not too particular about this, but this was just an opportunity to rid themselves of a months filth and even lice, but to feel slightly clean and refreshed once more. The men spent several nights being billeted within the large factory building, and had the added luxury of bunks to sleep upon, whilst they undertook logistical work within the town.

Francis and the Lincolnshire's endured two further posting's back to the front line, during the early months of 1916, and both postings were very similar to that first posting in December, as fortunately both were uneventful events, with only a few brief exchanges being experienced by either side, within this quiet sector. He would often be selected as part of a reconnaissance party and often venturing out into 'no man's land' during nighttime hours, as this was usually undertaken to repair any shell damaged barbed wire, that lay forward of the British trench.

It was now May and the weather had warmed significantly, which helped to make life somewhat more bearable on the front line. In the period following their third posting to the front line whist the men undertook recuperation in Albert, the Lincolnshire regiment were required to take part in a major logistical operation, involving the movement of arms and other such Military hardware, that were being stockpiled toward the rear of the front line positions. All of the work had to be undertaken during the nighttime hours, so as to avoid possible detection from any German surveillance. The logistical operation was undertaken over a two week period, as Francis and the others couldn't comprehend the vast quantities of equipment that were now being moved forward. Rumours soon passed between the men of a significant push that was about to happen very soon against the Germans. The objective being to drive them away from the valley of the River Somme, in an attempt to break through the western frontline. So much equipment was being stockpiled along the communication trenches, as it sat awaiting further movement forward. Here Francis noticed numerous automatic weapons and field guns that were being moved, to which he had earlier received full operational training whilst he was at Belton Park. This helped to further boost his mood, and at the thought that he might now be involved in their use.

Back at the billet, all of the men within Francis's group were ordered to line up, where ten men who looked to be the strongest and most heavily built were to be selected by an Officer, and were asked to follow the Officer outside. Due to his natural physique, Francis was possibly the first man to be selected from the group for this covert task, and so he was told to follow the Officer outside, along with the other selected men. Each man was then asked his occupation, as each one replied to the Officer, and all would typically highlight some physically demanding work role. They had all been selected to undertake an extension to the existing front line trench system, with the outcome being to enable the sighting of several additional 'fire steps,' at strategically placed positions, that would be able to cover a significant area of no man's land directly forward of the trench system. The men were then taken back over toward the front line, and for the first part of this journey they were taken by an Army truck, until they were forced to walk the remainder of the journey, as they neared toward the trench sector.

They were all instructed to report to the Officer at the sector command post, who walked with them toward the dig area, as he highlighted the direction, to which the new trench was now to be dug. He explained that all of the work had to be undertaken well out of sight from the German position that was less than ninety yards away, at this point in the trench system. All work had to be undertaken undetected and underneath the height of the trench parapet at all times, and to highlight no visible sign of any movement taking place. The task was made even more difficult, due to the fact of the earth being removed, had to be taken away from the dig in sacks, where they were used to assist with further fortifications, toward the rear of the trench system.

Francis and the selected men immediately set to the task of digging the trench, and divided themselves into smaller work groups, in order to organise the work. Three men were responsible for the actual digging, as three men working toward the rear of the diggers, were responsible for the shovelling of the dislodged earth into sack's, whilst the other four men carried the sacks away from the dig area, and were placed further back within the trench system.

The work was a hard undertaking, as the greatest difficulty was the avoidance of any detection from the German position, who would immediately shell the area, if anything unusual was suspected. The men were not allowed to smoke to avoid detection from the spent tobacco smoke, as they soon developed a robust working system. They were soon to develop a favoured way to remove the vulnerable surface level earth without detection. This involved digging at creating a cavity about eighteen inches below the earth surface, and after only a few feet of further digging, the surface earth would give way under its own weight, and fall undetected directly into the trench. The men took turns, as to the differing work roles involved in the dig, and worked through the heavy clay soil, made even more difficult to work, by not being able to work at the soil from above. Progress was made of around seven yards a day, of this newly extracted trench system as the June weather also turned quite warm during the period, as they toiled relentlessly slowly moving the earth.

On the fourth day of excavation, Francis and two other men were tasked with the digging into a pocket of loose stone shale that had been formed within the clay, and were required to use both picks and shovels during this heavy work of undercutting the surface earth. Suddenly Francis's pick head disappeared into a soft crevice within the shale of the earth wall. A faint rumbling noise could be heard, coving from the crevice, as a mass of 'black' now began to appear as if pouring from the pick hole. He could now see that they were Wasps, and that the pick had hit the nest of a large colony, the other men quickly reeled backwards from the disturbance, and managed to alert the others, as they ran back along the trench system, as thousands of disturbed and agitated Wasps began to appear from the hole. Francis would not be so fortunate, as he stumbled backward over a discarded pick and feel to the ground, he was quickly overcome by thousands of Wasps in their natural defence of the nest. Because of the warm conditions, none of the digging party had been wearing shirts, so Francis became a target for the agitated and stinging Wasps frantically circling this area of the trench in their agitated state, like a large black cloud. The men within the vicinity had now all moved away from this part of the trench, leaving Francis to the onslaught of the attacking Wasps. He lay and withered in agony at the mass of stinging that was being administered toward his head and upper body. He tried to climb back up to his feet, but was constantly slowed by the excruciating pain of the stings that were now covering his entire head and upper body. Another Soldier ran back down the trench toward Francis carrying a blanket, as he threw this over to him with a view to offering him some sort of protection, as many of the other men could only look on in horror and disbelief, unsure as to what they could do, to help him. He managed to pull the blanket over his upper body to cover himself, as he summoned the strength to run over toward the far side of the trench, where he collapsed to the floor in his agony. A few stray Wasps had followed him as they continued to attack him, and possibly due to the pheromone attraction being released from his stings. His face and body were both severely swollen, as the Commanding Officer immediately instructed him to be taken away for treatment, as two stretcher bearers were summoned to attend to him. As he was carried him out of the trench system, he screamed in agony on the stretcher, feeling every movement as the stretcher bearers negotiated the rough terrain of the trench floor.

Once out of the trench system, and hidden from the view of the German range, stood a waiting Army Ambulance placed in situ to carry any wounded away from this sector. The medic in attendance had no idea, as how to relieve Francis's severe discomfort and pain, as this was something he had never experienced before, so all he could administer were morphine phials, until they could get Francis to see a Doctor back at the dressing station. His pain was excruciating, as the Ambulance negotiated the bumpy unmade road back toward Albert and the dressing station, as the morphine did little to relieve his plight.

Once at the dressing station, he was taken inside a tent, and was placed onto a surgical table. The Army Doctor now examined both his head and body, but was forced to seek further advice from another colleague, outside of the tent. As he lay on the surgical table, the doctor then brought in a beaker simply containing white vinegar, and proceeded to dab the vinegar solution all over his head and body. Following this action he was quickly carried off into another tent, where two female Nurses, then proceeded to remove any infected heads of the deposited stings with tweezers, and again these were dabbed with the solution following their removal. It was later learned that Francis had endured over six hundred stings to both his upper body and head. This would be an agonising and dilapidating experience for any man, and possibly more due to his strength of physique he was able to survive this level of infection. He was then transferred to a much smaller tent, to where he was immobilised to a sick bed, along with five other injured Soldiers being cared for, within the tent.

Francis was nursed at this dressing station for over two weeks, and to enable his recovery back to some form full health and strength. During his first week at the station he had been unable to even walk given the severity of the stinging attack, and the effect that this had upon his nervous system. Thankfully he had no opportunity to see a reflection of himself within the tent during this difficult and painful experience but had been told by the others, that he had looked horrendous, with the level of infection and swelling being experienced within his head and body.

As he lay on his bed under the canvass of the tent, the relentless pounding of the large guns from both sides, could clearly be heard in the distance, as this enabled the men very little rest. He had heard from the other men, that a 'big push' against the German's positions was soon to be taking place. It was also quite noticeable that very little was seen of any of the medical staff during this period of activity, as rumours soon began to circulate the dressing station, as to the casualty rates being unimaginable. It would not be long before he was asked to vacate his bed, and he was to be transferred from the war zone to an area further west, in order for him to fully recuperate with the view to him eventually re-joining his unit. He was billeted in an old Chateau that had been commissioned by the Army, and the two weeks he spent there allowed him to recover both his walking ability, and to reintroduce sufficient movement to all of his limbs. The swelling and infection were now beginning to subside, as he began to feel much better in himself, possibly helped further by the warm August weather.

After the two week stay billeted at the Chateau, the Army Doctor had discharged him back to join his unit, as he signed the papers for his discharge, and with a view to him recommencing full duties with the regiment. Rumours had circulated the billet, about the carnage that had been experienced within the Somme area, but nothing could prepare Francis for the devastation and loss that was awaiting for him back in Albert.

On his return to Albert he reported to the command post, yet everything seemed to be in such a chaotic state, and so different from the regimented and organised calm of the place, that he had known only several weeks earlier. An Officer then informed him that most of the men he had served with in the Lincolnshire regiment, were possibly missing during the early days of the offensive, as the sector of trench to which they were posted had been heavily bombarded, in order to stem the British attacks across the sector. His company had been decimated, and it was explained to him that it was so fortunate that he had missed the outcome of the push as a result of him being so badly injured. He felt so numb at the receipt of this news, and to comprehended the losses of so many of the young men, he had barely known for less than a year, all now gone.

He was ordered to report to the Commanding Officer of the West Riding regiment, to whom he would now be attached for the remainder of the war. The West Riding men were being billeted on recuperation at an orchard, located about three miles to the west of Albert, having recently completed a posting to the front line. He was ordered to walk over to the orchard, as he was passed written directions from the Officer. It took Francis over an hour to reach the orchard, as he walked along the unmade lane toward the main Farmhouse. All seemed to be so quiet and not the usual noise to be expected from an Army billet. The Farmer in broken English directed Francis toward a large stone built Barn located toward the rear of the farmhouse, and yet everything was so quiet. He took in a deep breath composed himself and opened the small 'wicket' door of the Barn. The barn was lit, only by candlelight as Francis squirmed to see as his eyes adjusted to the darkness of the Barn. Toward the far side of the Barn could be seen several Soldiers, and all observing a card game, being played out by six other Soldiers.

"Who the fuck are you?", came a direct question from one of the group.

"Ive been attached to you lot" Francis responded.

"What unit?" the Soldier asked him.

"Lincolnshire" replied Francis.

Behind him an Officer had now entered the Barn, as the men quickly stood up to attention, leaving the card game in situ, as he called to them all at ease. Francis then introduced himself to the Officer, who asked what had been his experience with the Lincolnshire's. He explained he had received machine gun training at Belton Park, but as yet had not been able to demonstrate this.

"Excellent replied the Officer, we will pair you with Garvin, who has also been trained" he replied.

"Garvin, this is Francis he is joining us from the Lincolnshire's, show him the ropes, I will pair you two for the field gun."

Francis noticed that the Soldier who was participating in the card game, was the Soldier identified by the Officer, as Garvin.

Garvin then walked over to Francis as he held out his hand "Pleased to meet thi, I'm Sam, Sam Garvin, from Sheffield."

"William Francis from Boston" he replied shaking Garvin's hand.

"Fancy a game of cards?" asked Garvin.

Chapter 3 - Samuel Garvin.

Samuel Garvin, was born in Sheffield, Yorkshire in 1895 to Milburn and Emily Garvin, he was the younger of two brothers, and two younger sisters that made up the Garvin family. Soon after Samuel was born, the family moved to School Lane situated in the Park district of Sheffield, whilst his father gained work as a labourer in the loading of Canal Barges at the nearby Sheffield Basin. Samuel was always a difficult and rebellious child, and often in trouble with the authorities from as early as 1905. Around the age of ten, and following on from a beating being administered toward him by his teacher, Samuel chose to stop attending school altogether, and would spend his days hanging around with his older brother Robert, and his companions in the nearby city centre. His father not happy that both brothers weren't contributing anything toward the family income, threw both boys out of the family home. Having to survive at such an early age, both brothers had to quickly develop a degree of self-resilience, and soon became quite 'streetwise' within their new and often hostile surroundings.

Being too young to gain any regular employment, Samuel would supplement any meagre income by selling copies of the 'Sheffield Telegraph' newspaper from a pitch situated in Fitzalan Square, and of the occasional foray into stealing, and other such petty criminal activity. Samuel being the more intelligent of both Garvin brothers, and possibly enabled them both to evade capture for so long, as he would always scrutinise all probabilities in any such undertaking, before actually committing the offence. They both temporary lived in a derelict house located near to Campo Lane, and of them being such a young and vulnerable age, it wasn't long before several associates had, 'double crossed' them, and had swindled them out of money. Both quickly adapted, to become more resilient and cautious in all of their undertakings and associations. Scrap metal and coal theft was always a 'good earner' for the brothers on the streets of industrial Sheffield. They had soon acquired a discarded old pram to assist with the transportation of scrap metal and coal, to any willing customers. As their reputation grew, and of their potential to earn money, it was only a matter of time before they were both living back at home, and were now able to contribute toward the family income.

After a several years of this chaotic lifestyle, Samuel realised that he could earn more money through stealing, and the disposal of goods through several known associates, rather than take on a typical factory job in the many steelworks of Sheffield. It wasn't long before Robert would be apprehended by the Police, whilst undertaking a theft of lead gullies from a factory roof, although Samuel was not with him on this occasion, and Robert had typically undertaken the theft without any thought or forward planning. Samuel continued to evade capture, with his thorough and careful assessment of any job he was to undertake. Robert was sentenced to eighteen months hard labour, and therefore leaving more of a burden on the young Samuel to supplement the income of the family, as he further began to increase in his illegal undertakings, that was occasionally supplemented by illegal gambling.

At the outbreak of the 'Great War' in 1914, Samuel was nineteen years old, and him being of the prime age for recruitment into the armed forces. To overcome him being conscripted to the armed forces, at the outbreak of the war, he immediately took a job in one of the many Steelworks of the city working in a Rolling Mill that was busy manufacturing for the war effort, and was deemed to be in a 'reserved occupation' to avoid conscription. It wouldn't be too long before Samuel soon grew tired and bored of the hard manual labouring work in the Rolling

Mill, as he began to gravitate toward the 'Sky Edge,' gambling ring, rather than attend for work. He first worked as a lookout at 'Sky Edge' often known as a 'Pikey,' and soon he had become a trusted associate of another Park man, called Edward Wild, an illegal bookmaker who ran the whole gambling operation at 'Sky Edge.' Samuel soon worked his way within the hierarchy of the small group of men who looked after Edward Wild, and oversaw any matters at 'Sky Edge.' He soon realised that the money being earned at 'Sky Edge' to be much easier rather than having to work shifts, in a hot, dusty, noisy, and often dangerous Rolling Mill environment.

His employer at the Rolling Mill terminated his employment due to his continual absence, and immediately notified the authorities of this. He was soon being pursued by the War Office for his enlistment as they required his conscription into the armed forces. He was now being sought by the Police as he continued to evade capture, by travelling to various racecourses throughout Northern England with Edward Wild, and working as his Bookmakers Assistant. On their frequent returns back home to Sheffield, Garvin began to take more of an active interest in the operation at 'Sky Edge.' Edward Wild was now beginning to tire of 'Sky Edge,' as he realised, that there were more lucrative earnings to be made, on the racecourses of Northern England.

With 'Sky Edge' being located so near to the heart of the Park district, Garvin was soon to be assisted by many of his local friends and associates, whom he had known since his childhood. George Mooney was such a man, as Garvin had known him for a number of years, although he was not from the Park district, he had been a regular and a trusted associate of Edward Wild, and he soon became a key member involved within the operation at 'Sky Edge.' Mooney and several of the other Park men looked after the undertakings of 'Sky Edge,' as Garvin continued to evade enlistment by frequently travelling with Edward Wild, but it would only be a matter of time before Garvin would be apprehended, as the 'Great War' gathered in its momentum.

It was well known that Sam Garvin could be a ruthless, and often violent individual, and on one such occasion he was foolishly arrested at the Haydock Park racecourse. He was arrested with the charge of 'common assault against the person,' this had been committed upon a man who had contested the payout given to him by Edward Wild. Following his arrest he was remanded and due to appear at the Warrington Assizes on the following day as a result of the assault charge. As his identity was established, the Military Police were contacted and he was immediately escorted by the Military Police to the Catterick Garrison in north Yorkshire. After evading enlistment for so long he was now drafted into the Army and to begin his basic training. The Military Police now held the man who had evaded them for so long, and it was agreed by the Judiciary his trial at Warrington Assizes, was to be placed on hold, until the completion of his Army service.

Although reluctant, Garvin soon settled into Army life and enjoyed much of training instruction. After six weeks of his basic Army training at the Catterick Garrison, he would then be posted to North Wales for further battlefield training, as he was enlisted into the West Riding Field Gun regiment. He soon learned that the regiment were to be deployed over to Northern France. It was now June 1916, and all men from his regiment were to be granted a forty-eight hour leave pass, before their disembarkation to France, all with the exception of Garvin. He was ordered to remain at the camp, for fear of his desertion, should he return back to Sheffield.

Being so angry at his Commanding Officers for their part in enforcing this ban, he quickly changed in his compliance toward the Army, and until that point had shown some promise in his making as a Soldier. At his disappointment to this news and totally unprovoked, he attempted to attack another Soldier at the camp, with an expectation of an immediate Court Martial. But much to his own surprise, the Commanding Officers at the camp would not react to the provocation demonstrated byGarvin, In their viewpoint all available men were desperately required at the 'Western Front,' to initiate a 'big push' that was forthcoming against the German front line. So the assault charges brought against Garvin, were subsequently dropped.

On the Monday morning of June 5th 1916, Garvin's company of the West Riding regiment departed from Chester Railway Station, and were bound for London, with onward travel toward Folkestone. Like many other men on the train, Garvin put on a brave front to disguise his own concern at the prospect of what they were all to find over in France. They jokingly played cards, and fooled around on the train. Stories had circulated back at the camp, as to the many horrors of the warfare to be experienced in France. But like the rest of the men in this situation, Garvin hoped that this might just be over exaggeration on the part of those who had relayed the stories.

They men had arrived at Folkestone harbour at around six o clock on that evening, and were immediately ushered on board what looked to be a cross channel Ferryboat. The Ferryboat was crammed full with Soldiers, and there was little space available on any of the decks, whilst Garvin and his immediate comrades found a quiet corner of the upper deck, where they were able to sit on their back packs. The journey across the English Channel to France took them around three hours, and the Ferryboat was escorted by two Royal Navy destroyers, sailing to either side of the Ferryboat during the calm crossing. As they sat and watched the white cliffs, and the coastline of England slowly disappear into the distance, and being reflected so brightly by the evening sun. Many men now began to realise that after the past few weeks of training, this was now the 'real event,' and not the 'phoney war' as was all being experienced back at home. This would now be the actual opportunity to face, and kill the enemy. The boat journey across the Channel was relatively calm, and the risk of any U. Boat attack, being so minimised by the presence of the Royal Navy destroyers.

The Ferryboat docked in Boulogne, as the men disembarked they were all directed over to an Army train that was stood waiting adjacent to the quayside. Following disembarkation, the train, it was soon leaving the port of Boulogne fully loaded, and heading into the French countryside. Nightfall was beginning to descend, and the only difference that was noticeable from the train journey they had experienced down to Folkestone, were the regular flashes which frequently lit up the night sky overhead.

The train travelled through the stark darkness of the French countryside for around two hours, frequently illuminated by bright flashes of light as it slowed to a halt, at an unmarked and faintly lit railway station, where the men were all ordered off the train. They were instructed to form into a groups within their appropriate companies. As each company gathered, they were allocated to a single Officer, and told to follow the individual Officer, toward a line of waiting trucks. None of the men had eaten anything since the food stall back at Waterloo Station, and had no idea as to where they were now being taken. After around thirty minutes of travelling in convoy along a narrow road the trucks came to a halt outside what appeared to be a large Church in a small village, as the men were ordered inside the Church. The continual flashes of light and the sound of explosives could now clearly be heard in the near distance, and once inside the Church building, they were served with bacon and cut bread, from the line of stoves located along one side of the large hall. Garvin then asked one of the catering Soldiers as to where they were, as he replied by telling him Doulens. This meant nothing to Garvin, and they would be no doubt informed more on the following day. After the bacon, bread and tea, the company were ordered outside, and once more instructed to follow the Officer toward the rear of the Church, where the men were to be billeted, inside a large old brick built Barn. Several piercing screeches were then heard overhead, to which many of the men quickly ducked down, and much to the amusement of several men who were already billeted inside the Barn and laid on the straw bales in makeshift beds. Garvin and several his comrades, moved around the large Barn, and quickly struck up a conversation with one of the Soldiers, who had already been billeted there.

"Where are we?" one of the men asked.

"Doulens in Picardie" the Soldier replied to him.

"Are we near the front line?" Garvin asked him.

"Afraid so mate, its about 8 miles that way," pointing toward the gable end of the Barn.

He continued "Not too bad over here, at least we are not in tents, something big is happening soon, though, probably why you lot are all here, I've never seen as many shells and guns, being moved around before."

"Are there trenches here?" asked Garvin

"Yes, on the lower ground, some were German trenches that we took over, there are gun positions dotted on the higher ground, and this overlooks the Germans, they won't attack there" he replied.

The continual sound of screeching and loud explosions filled the warm night air outside the Barn, as Garvin like the other newly arrived men got very little sleep on that first night, so worried that a shell might strike the Barn, at any time. Candles were alight at various locations throughout the barn, and unable to sleep he had decided to write a letter back home, to let them know of his safe arrival in France. He was still feeling bitter at not being able to see his family before he had left for France, but began to take comfort in the fact, that he had evaded enlistment for so long prior to this, and hopefully the war might well be over soon. He had a pencil in his backpack, and managed to source a piece of paper from another Soldier, who advised him before he wrote, not to mention any location in the letter, and just keep this to France, otherwise the letter would be destroyed.

The following morning, the weary men were woken at six o clock and told to report to the church for breakfast, yet more bacon and bread with hot tea, but at least this was hot food. They finished breakfast and waited outside the church, in the warm morning of the late June sunshine. Garvin observed the shellfire damaged houses of the village, and the rubble which littered either side of the roadway. The men were told to line up, as each section of the company undertook a roll call, following which they were addressed by the Commanding Officer. He told them they were to undertake a route march of around fifteen miles, to a location southward, where they were to camp that night. The company lined up at 'four men abreast' and began the march, all were in peak physical condition, following their basic training back in England. The day was already quite warm and sunny, as the miles began to pass, marching at a regular pace. Around two hours later, the instruction was given to rest and to take on water from a nearby stream, this rest stop lasted for around fifteen minutes before the orders were given to continue with the march. The Commanding Officer had now joined the company on the march, as he had acquired a horse, as he quickly galloped toward the front of the company to take the lead. By twelve noon the company had reached the camp site, and all were ordered at ease, and directed toward the field kitchen tent to pick up their rations, this time it was bully beef and bread, with the customary hot tea.

Whilst at the camp, during the following days the men were put to work with the loading and movement of small ordnance, being taken from large Army trucks and loaded onto much smaller carts, as these were being transported toward the front line, and pulled along by horses. The work was heavy and relentless, in the warm June sun. The only relief to the heat, was a large horse stone troft to which the men would often submerge themselves to cool themselves, between deliveries. They all suspected that something big would be happening, and of the war now gathering momentum, as to what the Soldier back at the mess in Doulens had mentioned. As work for the day had ended, and before they were dismissed for their evening rations in the field kitchen, a young Officer approached the group and requested their attention, as he then addressed the group. He calmly relayed to the company that a major offensive was about to be undertaken by the allies and beginning at dawn on the following morning. The West Riding regiment were to be included in a second wave of attack being led toward German positions near to Theipval. All of the men including Garvin, now revelled in their excitement at the prospect of actually fighting, and being able to fire their guns toward the enemy. As they were newly arrived, they had little experience of the realities of life in the trenches, or of what was to be expected of them. As they sat and ate their rations several men highlighted were now just simply relieved, not have to be involved any more in the hard work of the logistical operation. Many men lay awake that night being unable to sleep in the anticipation of the front line assault, but relayed the possible reality that this push, might actually end the war.

All were disturbed from any scarce sleep they had managed at around three thirty on that following morning, by an intense barrage of a shell bombardment, that was happening at a location quite near to them. If the men weren't nervous before, the continual relentless noise of the bombardment was so deafening, as shell, after shell exploded. At exactly four o clock two gigantic explosions were heard as each violently vibrated through the earth of the camp, such was their intensity. The relentless noise caused some of the men to be temporary deafened as a direct result of the explosions.

Reveille then sounded, and it could be hardly heard against the noise of the continual bombardment in the distance, as a hastily held roll call was then undertaken, before they were instructed to go for breakfast. After breakfast, all were ordered to pack up their kit bags and to move toward the roadside where only the previous day they had been busy loading the small ordnance. A marching order was given by the lead Officer, as the West Riding men moved forward on their route toward the front line. The bombardment had now subsided, as a coronet player accompanied the men on the march, and many popular tunes were requested from down the line, accompanied by singing as they marched. Nothing could be seen of the front line that awaited them from the road, but several explosions and the sound of rapid gunfire could now clearly be heard. The men were ordered to halt, at a small path that ran at a right angle from the road, through some shell damaged woodland and led toward the direction of the front line sector. The path then dropped down between a hollow, and into an area of enclosed grassland. The men followed the Officer in a single line and downward into the hollow, as they climbed the opposite side of the hollow, a large shell exploded immediately toward the left of their position. The noise deafened most of the men for several seconds, and Garvin was hit with a small piece of stone from the blast which caused him some bleeding to his forehead, but after recomposing himself he was fine to continue toward the front line. The men continued to climb the hollow, and cut into the small hillside were the beginning of the rear service trenches, and leading down into the main trench system. As the men descended into the trench system, Garvin was so curious as to what lay over this small hill, as the image he viewed just startled him, as he looked out over 'no man's land' and toward the German positions. A mass of men, smoke, explosions and fires could be observed, stretching for miles in either direction. He quickly followed the other men and descended into the relative safety of the deeper trenches, he could hear the clink of live bullets, now ricocheting above the parapet. The men moved forward toward the front line, the trench floor was pretty dry and easy going, considering the recent warm conditions, but what was noticeable was the lack of any other Army personal within the trench. The first wave of attack had already left the trench earlier that morning, and the West Riding's were now to wait until two o clock for the signal for the second wave to attack. It was now midday as the men leant up against the trench wall waiting for their signal, some sat underneath the home made ladders, to try to offer some form of protection from the regular explosions of flying earth and shrapnel.

Before long, Garvin noticed that several Soldiers were now beginning to drop back down into the trench, from over the parapet and 'no mans land.' Many were in a state of panic as they ran back toward the direction of the service trenches. Some were quite badly injured, as the West Riding men then rushed forward to assist them in whatever way they could help, before several stretcher bearers appeared. This soon changed the outlook of the men, from that earlier enthusiasm, to one of shock and now a possible anticipation of their own fate. Garvin looked on, as he was unable to help a young man possibly only seventeen or eighteen years old, loose his fight directly in front of him.

Garvin had been paired with a man called Tommy Fieldsend who had hailed from Wakefield. Both had been trained in the use of a field gun whilst they were stationed in North Wales, as they were ordered to keep together in the advance, as one man was to carry the field gun, whilst the other carried the bullet belts. An Officer asked them both to follow him toward the sector command post, where they were to pick up the automatic weapon, and the bullets. Fieldsend offered to carry the gun, so that Garvin loaded up the heavy bullet belts around his body in anticipation of the signal to advance.

In a repeat of the offensive that had happened earlier on that morning at around one thirty, an intense barrage of shells was launched that were to pepper the German front lines of this sector, before the West Ridings were ordered to advance. On this occasion the barrage would only last for around ten minutes. He couldn't help but to think of the possibly that several British Soldiers from that first wave, were possibly caught up in the vicinity of the bombardment, by our own shelling. As they waited anxiously to advance more men appeared to be dropping back down into the trench system, all in a variety of either distressed states or injury, this had quite an unsettling effect upon the men, as the time neared for the West Riding's to advance over the parapet. A Corporal walked down the line of men, giving each man a drink from a small ladle that contained rum, this gave Garvin a warming feeling inside of him, and helped to put himself a little more at ease for what he was about to face.

At exactly two o clock the charge whistles sounded along the trench, to order the advance, as Garvin and Fieldsend climbed up the makeshift ladder, into an intensity of smoke, chaos and noise all around them, as they slowly moved forward toward the direction of the German positions. At this point of entering 'no mans land' they had no idea as to where the German positions or guns were located. As both men simply hoped to pick up on their position from the direction of bullets flying toward the advancing party. They walked haphazardly over the peppered and uneven ground, as the stench of sulphur and burning from the small fires, that were everywhere, and still nothing could be seen of the enemy positions through the drifting smoke. Suddenly a barrage of bullets passed toward their left side, and hitting several men in the process. He suddenly flinched at this action, as both men slowly continued with their advance, bearing the weight of both the field gun and of the bullet belts. Fieldsend now estimated that they were possibly around three hundred yards from the German positions, and so could be within easy range of their snipers, and this was possibly only being avoided due to the intense smoke from the fires that were shielding them. They spotted a shallow shell hole, and both decided to set up the field gun, with a view to covering a German gun post that had now been located by them, and was firing directly from their right side.

The gun field gun was quickly assembled and as they had anticipated, the shell hole proved to be elusive to the German snipers. They were able to hold this position and to quieten the German gun until later that evening, when they eventually ran out of bullets. Their position had allowed for many of the West Riding's to enter this part of the German trench system under the cover of the field gun, and to take several German prisoners as a direct result. Garvin and Fieldsend had now ceased firing due to no ammunition remaining, the German machine gun post suddenly reverberated back into life, and once more had this particular area of 'no mans land' covered within its sights. The men who had earlier entered the German trench system, were now unable to continue with the further securing of this sector. Garvin now volunteered to go back toward the British trench for more ammunition, with the outcome to continue with subduing of the German gun, and to allow another attack.

A mortar shell exploded directly in front of both men, covering them with earth and other such debris, Garvin then saw this as the opportunity to move from the shell hole. Without hesitation he sprinted the four hundred yards back toward the British trench. Smoke was still rising from the exploded mortar shell, which helped to shield his position from the German machine gun post. He ran for all his life, as he began to sprint in the 'zig zag' formation back toward the British trench across the uneven ground. Within several seconds the German field gunner spotted Garvin, as he could now hear bullets closely whizz by him. The wire above the British trench had been cut in several places to allow for the advancement earlier in the day, and as he approached the wire, he knew the German gunner would have his sights now trained upon this gap, but to his amazement he ran through, and dived down into the safety of the trench.

Landing on his shoulder in an attempt to break his fall on the trench floor, he was slightly hurt but was able to stand and to find his way toward the sector command post. He explained their predicament to the Commanding Officer, and roughly drew the position of the machine gun post over a map. The Officer then sent another man toward the rear of the trench system, where a single cannon was located. The outcome being to bombard this troublesome machine gun position, and to cover Garvin and another man, who were to return back toward the shell hole with him, both fully laden with bullet belts. The bombardment would be timed for ten minutes time at six forty, and further allowed for Garvin to take on water, and carry a small container for Fieldsend, back at the shell hole. As the shells began to explode in the vicinity of the German gun post, both men climbed over the parapet, and sprinted toward the shell hole, with both men taking an alternating 'zig zag' formation, through the 'no mans land.'

No bullets were fired toward their direction, until they were around fifteen yards from the shell hole with Garvin leaping forward and taking a dive into the relative safety of the shell hole. The other Soldier was not so lucky, as Garvin turned and watched him being cut to pieces, as he was peppered by bullets being relentlessly fired from the German gun. Fieldsend then quickly managed to reload the field gun, and again the German gun post was silenced. This allowed for more men to move forward and beyond the German wire, and soon an explosion could be seen coming from the direction of the German gun post. Fieldsend silenced his own gun, and no fire was observed being returned from the German gun. Garvin reasoned with him that they should remain there until nightfall, and return back to the British trench in the cover of darkness. Yet Fieldsend was confident the post had now been captured. As he rose up to his feet for a closer inspection, within seconds he was directly hit by a sniper, and fell backward onto the crouching Garvin. He was killed instantly, with the single shot as Garvin attempted to push Fieldsend off himself, as his warm blood now soaked onto his face and uniform. Garvin lay there motionless, unable to move or even to breathe properly, as he listened to the madness happening all around him. Although the July evening air was warm, he felt cold as he shivered and trembled in his wait until nightfall and of complete darkness, with both dead men now laid within his immediate vicinity.

Darkness had now shrouded the battlefield, and in the brief dark period between the light of flares, he managed to sprint back toward the British trench, and as he had done earlier that day, unseen by any snipers, he reached the cut section of the British wire, and dived back into the trench. He re-composed himself, and then reported to the sector command, to relay the information of the death of Fieldsend and of the other Soldier. He met with the same Officer who had ordered the bombardment earlier, who regardless of the death of both men, immediately went on to ask him "where was the field gun?"

Garvin was dismayed at this question, as the regiment had probably lost hundreds of men, in this offensive on that day, and all this Officer seemed to be concerned about was the abandonment of a field gun. He was asked for his Army number by the Officer, and told he was to be placed on a charge, and to be dealt with later. Things soon quietened within the sector, following the carnage of that first day, with much of the German sector within this area was now destroyed, and abandoned. What truly desponded Garvin, was the lack of any further advancement taken during the days following on from the attack, and the West Riding men were now ordered to defend the trench from further attack. He could not comprehend as to why they were not advancing further. He was so angry at the thought of the men who had been lost and maimed in the offensive, and for this lack of advancement by his unit, all for no reason.

He barely knew any of the men now within his sector, and so he assumed that many of the comrades he had known earlier, had been lost. The West Riding's spent five more disillusioned and uneventful days in the trench, until they were relieved by the Durham Infantry. They marched back toward a new camp at a Farm near to Albert where they were to be billeted over the next few days. It was so noticeable at the reduction in the number of men, compared to those who had marched in the opposite direction on this same road, only six days earlier. The West Riding men reached the Farm that was located within a large Orchard, where they were to be billeted in a Barn, located toward the rear of the Farmhouse, where they were to undergo ten days recuperation, before being sent back to the front line.

Chapter 5 - A.W.O.L.

Garvin and Francis hastily slipped away from the rest of the unit, by running down an alleyway adjacent to a Church in a small village they were passing through, none of the other men had noticed them disappear. The alleyway led them directly into a small courtyard, where a Cooper was sat outside his workshop, working on a half made wooden barrel, as the Cooper just sat staring at both men. They leaped over a small wooden fence located toward the rear side of the courtyard, and into a recently ploughed crop field where they ran quickly across the open field, to woodland located at the opposite side. The Cooper just sat silently and stared at both Soldiers, as they disappeared into the woodland, as he then continued with his work.

With the stolen map in their possession, they had highlighted that the woodland would eventually lead them toward the railway line linking Dieppe on the coast, to Amiens. The weather was mild and dry, so they were able to make good progress, in the fading light of the dusk. After about thirty minutes of steady running, they had reached the main rail line, and began to follow the track bed in the direction of Dieppe. A Train could be heard approaching in the distance, as both men ran down the steep embankment, and crouched in the undergrowth, as the Train passed above them. It was then suggested by Garvin, that it might be best to rest there until complete darkness, and to continue the journey toward Dieppe, after sunset.

As darkness fell, both men moved quickly along the rail line, and realised that by now, both would have been highlighted as missing by the regiment. It was important that they moved quickly, and so as not to be spotted within the wide open and flat countryside of the Pas de Calais region. They both had agreed to keep moving all night, with the minimum of delay, and to find somewhere to rest at day break. No trains passed them during the nighttime, and was possibly due to the fact of German guns identifying any movement of light from their position on the higher ground several miles away, and were possibly still within their range.

As day light began to reappear, they noticed a small open sided barn, located to the right of the rail line, which looked to be an ideal place for much needed rest during the daytime. Garvin anticipated that they had probably covered around thirty to thirty-five miles during that first night. The barn was open on all four sides, and was piled high with stacks of straw bales. They both climbed up onto the bales, where they sat and ate the remainder of their rations, as they tried to get some much needed sleep. Their adrenalin was so heightened, that as soon as they descended into any deep slumber, they quickly awakened at the thought of capture by the Military Police, and of their sub conscious highlighted reaction to any sounds coming from the outside of the barn. It wasn't a restful day for either of the men, with Garvin was getting so frustrated and wanting to continue their journey toward Dieppe. Francis always being the more cautious of the pair, persuaded Garvin of the danger of being so easily spotted within the wide open countryside in daylight. Several trains could be seen passing from the barn, clambering on their way back and forth between Dieppe and Amiens. Some of the trains were made up of passenger carriages, often crammed full with Soldiers, whilst others towed long rolling platforms carrying field guns and other such Military hardware, no doubt all made in Sheffield as was commented on by Garvin each time one passed by.

It was obvious to Francis that Garvin was getting frustrated and impatient, just for him to be sat around and waiting for dark fall.

The day endlessly dragged on, and as the skies began to darken for nightfall, rain began to fall.

"Is that bleeding typical, all day we are sat inside and its fuckin dry, and now we get soaked, this'll slow us" Garvin angrily reacted.

The rain now began to fall heavier, as both men quite stiff from the day's inactivity, climbed down from the barn, and moved back toward the railway line. The sky now darkened, and under the protection of their fatigue capes, they continued with their journey, the rain dripping off the capes and now began to soak through their trousers as they moved. Garvin pushed them both on, with Francis having to constantly keep up with him, he seemed to be like a man possessed in his attempt to reach Dieppe, and hopefully board a boat back over to England. They walked briskly all night, but this time they passed through the railway stations of two small villages located along the rail line. Both stations were in total darkness, and this being much to their advantage, but were still cautious as to the posting of any Sentries on guard duty at either of these stations. They passed through quietly and unchallenged, not seen by anyone. The rain had then ceased during the early hours of the morning, and both men disheveled, wet, and cold, were on the lookout for another place to sleep for the daytime hours. Francis was quite certain that they were now near to the coast, as he stated that he could smell the 'salt air,' and this helped to lighten the mood of Garvin as they continued. Francis checked his watch and it was already showing five o clock, and they had to find somewhere to shelter before the daylight came. Nowhere could be seen in the barren and flat landscape of the patchwork of fields. Francis suggested they had no alternative, but to hide down the bank of a drainage dyke located between two fields. Both men then left the railway line, and walked along the top of a dyke that transversed to the direction of the railway line. They had reached an intersecting dyke, to which they now climbed down, as both lay against the steep sides of the dyke, out of sight of the railway line. The drainage dyke was rather like a trench, about eight feet deep, eight feet wide at the top, and narrowing to about two feet wide, and a foot depth of water at the bottom. The overnight rain had ensured that the dyke walls were wet, but this quite reminded Francis of being at home in the Lincolnshire Fens. Francis then straddled and walked along the dyke floor collecting bull reeds, and other such foliage, as he proceeded to roll and tie these into a thick round ball shape. He placed several of these into the water of the dyke below to where Garvin was stood, and being much to the bewilderment of him.

"Now stand on the reeds" said Francis to Garvin.

As he duly obliged, he was amazed as to how this supported his weight and allowed him to stand upright and he was able to lay onto the side of the steep dyke bank wall, and without his feet slipping down into the water. Francis soon created another three reed balls, and now both men had a sufficient standing area, above the shallow water of the dyke. Before they settled down for some much needed rest. Francis also suggested they also cut some further reeds as camouflage, in the avoidance of being spotted from above by any Flying Corps planes, or other such surveillance.

Although they were possibly now over sixty miles away from the front line, the sound of exploding shells could still be clearly heard in the distance. Unlike on the previous day, both men were soon fast asleep in the warm air of the summer day, and were only awoken by Garvin slipping off the reed platform, and his feet dropping into the water, as both men quickly laughed off the incident following the cursing from Garvin. They could hear several more trains pass by, but this time they all sounding a whistle as they passed, this highlighted to them that the train was possibly approaching a junction, or even a nearby railway station, but according to they're reckoning, nothing was highlighted on the map between here and Dieppe. According to the map they were now about fifteen miles outside of Dieppe, the railway line at this point ran in a parallel direction to the coast. They both discussed the possibilities of either going across country, and then following the coast into Dieppe, or to stay on the railway line, and to move as close to Dieppe as was possible. Both were under the impression that once at Dieppe, they would be able to blend in with the Soldiers and Sailors, both arriving and disembarking through the port.

By nightfall both had agreed to continue and follow the rail line, but as to why the trains were all sounding their whistles at this point, was unknown. They followed the course of the dyke back toward the rail line. As the darkness began to fall, the sound of the shellfire from the frontline could again be clearly heard in the still night air, as they proceeded toward Dieppe. The rail line now began to curve in a leftward direction, as several small lights could be seen in the distance, to which all seemed to be adjacent to the rail line. Garvin was keen to push on, and to get nearer to whatever the source of the lights were, yet Francis always being the more cautious, was quite concerned as to whatever this unknown distraction was. There was no way both men could now continue along the railway line, so they attempted to take a detour around the adjacent fields, and to rejoin the railway line beyond the lights. As they left the rail line for the detour, both had noticed that a large and distinct shadow could be seen in the half moonlight, further along the railway line. Garvin was keen to investigate this further, and of the possibility of food or anything of further use to them. Rather than run the risk of both being apprehended. Garvin left his backpack with Francis, and proceeded back across the fields toward the direction of the rail line. Upon closer inspection, the shadow was of a stationary train with several carriages, stood waiting for disembarkation, and pointing toward the direction of Dieppe. There was no rear guard carriage attached to the train, so he was able to move down the carriages for a closer inspection. Although the carriages were in total darkness and appeared to be standard cargo carriages, he could clearly hear men's voices coming from inside the carriages. He headed back toward the rear carriage, and to his amazement he was able to gently slide open a door leading into the cargo hold. He climbed into the cargo hold, and found numerous sacks, all piled up to the roof of the carriage. He thought this would be an ideal opportunity for them to both stow away, for the short journey into Dieppe, and of a possible direct access to the port area. He quickly alighted from the cargo hold, as he hastily ran back over the fields, to where Francis was sat waiting, and told him of the discovery. Naturally Francis was quite reluctant to take up this offer at first, but was soon persuaded by Garvin, due to the unknown difficulties they might experience in trying to access the port at Dieppe by either road or land. Trains, he explained to Francis would probably be allowed direct access to the port area, and where both men could make further progress, in their goal of reaching England.

Both men hid away their rucksacks, within some nearby bushes, as they made their way across the open fields, toward the stationary train. They quietly climbed aboard and into the cargo hold, slowly closing the sliding door behind them. Francis briefly lit a match to highlight what else was in the hold, and it was revealed to be mail sacks, all destined for England. The smell from the sulphur of the match was soon overcome, from a putrid smell coming from four wooden packing cases that were located toward the rear of the hold, as one could be seen as leaking its contents onto the sawdust of the carriage floor. From the smell, and size of the packing cases, it was assumed that these were bodies, and possibly of Officers being repatriated back to England. Although the smell in such a confined space, made both men wretch and want to be sick, this was something they had to quickly overcome. Both buried themselves under the mail bags to hide, which also helped to relieve some of the odour being emitted from the packing cases.

Both men remained as silent as was possible, as voices could now be heard coming from the outside of the cargo hold, but no one entered the carriage. After about thirty minutes, they could hear the distinct sound of the steam engine being brought back into life, with the odd vibration now being felt throughout the carriage. Within minutes the customary whistle could be heard, and then the heightened sound of the release of steam, as the carriage now jolted forward. It slowly moved, as Francis realised he had a knot hole in the timber cladding of the cargo hold, and so was able to have a limited view of their surroundings. The train pulled slowly forward, and within only minutes had pulled up directly within a gas lit area of a hard standing. He could see several rows of shadows in the faint light, as the train came to a halt, after the brief movement forward. Francis could see, that he shadows were of men, some laid out on stretches, whilst others were either sat, or stood up. Beyond the lines of the men, could be seen several lines of tents that stretched away into the distance. The doors of the cargo holds further along the train could be heard sliding open, as the men on the stretches were now being loaded up onto the train, and were soon being followed onboard by the able bodied men, this looked to be a dressing station for injured troops, and were possibly being returned back to England. Francis whispered this information over to Garvin whilst they sat buried under the mail sacks, when suddenly the carriage door was slid open, as two more packing cases were roughly slid across the carriage floor. Just as quickly as it had opened, the door slid loudly shut behind them, as the whistle sounded and once more the train jolted forward.

What fate would now await both fugitives, and was only a matter of luck on their part, if they were able to sneak into Dieppe unnoticed, in their attempt to board a vessel bound for England. Both could now feel the train moving forward, and it was soon making good speed on its journey toward Dieppe. Around thirty minutes later they could feel that the train begin to slow, as both men soon realised this was now their fate, the risk of capture, or embarkation into the unknown. Confident that no other access would be made into their carriage until it came to a halt, Garvin peered through the gaps of the wood cladding, in his attempt to observe their position, and to contemplate for their next move. Both men could feel the train was now slowing to a standstill, and came to a halt adjacent to a large ship that was berthed in what they both assumed to be Dieppe harbour. As the train now halted, both men hid nervously behind the numerous mail sacks within the carriage, and awaited an opportunity to alight.

Several voices and the background noise of intense activity could now be clearly heard to the outside of the carriage, and Francis could see through the knot hole that the injured men were now being unloaded from the train, although the quayside was still in semi darkness, there were so many other people around, with the quayside so busy with activity. This would be the ideal opportunity to disappear into this hive of activity, and to possibly be unnoticed. Francis cautiously and slowly slid open the carriage door, and the fresh air of outside being such a relief to the putrid smell of rotting corpses, that had been in their company for the past fifteen or so miles. The quayside as expected was such a 'hive of activity,' even at this early hour of the morning, with both cargo and injured men, being loaded up the gang planks of the berthed boat. As they jumped down from the carriage, Garvin quickly grabbed a mail sack from the hold, and threw this over his shoulder with the view to carrying the mail sack and highlighted by nodding at Francis, to do the same. No one had noticed them both alighting from the carriage amongst the chaos of the quayside As both men carried a large mail sack each, and haphazardly negotiated the quayside, avoiding the many injured men laid out on stretches on the ground, and other such obstacles. They walked to the nearest gangplank of the boat, as they followed a line of around ten injured Soldiers walking up the gangplank, all with varying wounds but capable to walk unaided onto the boat. As they approached the top of the gangplank they were suddenly stopped by a civilian Stevedore

"Sorry boss, thought we could get these on quicker this way" replied Garvin, jokingly to the Stevedore.

At this vantage point of the boat, he could now see that there were another two gangplanks situated further along the boat, and all reaching down to the quayside. Toward the rear of the boat, could be seen a large steam operated crane, busy lifting cargo from the quayside up toward the deck, and the hoisted cargo then disappearing through a large hatch door into the hold below the rear deck. Both men now realised that the Stevedore had directed them, toward the rear gangplank, as unbeknown this was only being used for cargo. As they both turned around, the Stevedore then shouted for no more men to come up on board, as to allow for Garvin and Francis some space to be able to turn, and walk back down the gangplank, and onto the quayside. They could have well done without the attention now being drawn toward them, as they both hastily proceeded toward the stern of the boat with the mail bags. As they neared toward the stern, the noise and bustle of activity seemed to increase, here they also noticed injured men were being carried up onto the rear gangplank by the stretcher bearers, with the continual noise from the steam crane, sometimes quite deafening.

This was much to their favour, as they were unnoticed in the activity and queued up behind the line of stretcher bearers, eventually making their way up the gangplank carrying the mail sacks. One of the Soldiers laid on a stretcher in the queue, asked if Garvin would light him a cigarette, to which he reached into his pocket, and duly obliged, "Poor sod" Garvin was heard to say quietly to himself, as they both now walked up the gangplank. Another civilian Stevedore was monitoring the cargo coming on board, he was stationed at the top of this rear gangplank, and he was fluent in French also overseeing the French dock hands, bringing other cargo onboard.

"What's in those?" he asked Garvin.

"Mail sacks, what do you fucking think they are" was sarcastically responded by Garvin.

"OK mate, I can't see much in this light, put em in the rear hold, down those stairs" he replied, and pointing to an opened hatch door, underneath of which was a steep set of metal stairs.

Both men proceeded down the steep metal stairs, and into a vast cargo hold, where they dumped the mail sacks against the internal wall of the hull. There were around six others working inside the cargo hold, busy stacking and carrying the associated cargo, that was being loaded into the boat by the steam crane. They were all civilian men and it could be clearly heard, that all were French. Garvin then hit upon the idea of loading more mail sacks, so as not raise further suspicion as to them being inside the hold and to actively be seen as part of the loading operation, in the chaos of the quayside. Francis was content just to hide somewhere inside the hold, they had both got this far and to hopefully jump ship once they were back in England. Garvin thought that this undertaking, would avoid them any further suspicion as to them being on the boat, and this could possibly assist further upon their arrival in England. They both undertook several trips back to the train in the chaos of the quayside, and loaded more mail sacks onto the vessel.

By now, they were both on regular talking terms with the Stevedore stationed at the top of the rear gangplank, and were soon participating in the occasional brief cigarette break, and had developed a friendly rapport with him. They learnt from him, that the boat was destined for Southampton and was to be sailing at three o clock on that morning. It was now two fifteen, and another five sacks were required to be unloaded from the train, and soon only the six packing cases were remaining in the carriage of the train.

Both men realised that to unload these packing cases, might be subject to further scrutiny from Officers posted at the quayside, and they wanted to remain as discreet as was possible, so these were simply left inside the carriage, and the sliding door was closed. Several other Stevedore's now also began to acknowledge their presence in the cargo hold of the boat, and it had appeared that no one had cast any suspicion upon both men, as both were possibly assumed to be part of the Logistics Corps. The loading of the boat was now completed, and the large hatch into which the crane had earlier lowered cargo, was now closed up and bolted shut. The cargo hold was soon deserted as the French deckhands had now left the ship. The closing of the main cargo hatch shut away both the noise and chaos of the activity outside on the quayside, as everything seemed to become so quiet.

The Stevedore, to whom they had both been in brief conversation earlier, now appeared inside the hold as he then invited both men into a small and windowless room toward the far side of the cargo hold, where he offered them both a cup of tea. Inside the room were a table and six metal chairs, he disappeared out of the room, but had soon returned carrying a 'mashing can,' that was full of boiling water, in which to make the tea. Both men quickly drank the tea, although it was hot, and this being their first warm digestion for over three days, as they both began to feel relaxed.

Garvin then concocted up a story to the Stevedore, about him and Francis escorting the bodies of the dead Officers to Dieppe, but an Officer had asked them to participate in the loading procedure of the mail. They were both now to travel over to Southampton, and to then re-join the Logistics Corps back in Portsmouth, the Stevedore seemed so convinced at his story, as he again left the room to go and find both men some food from the galley.

They also learnt from the Stevedore, that the ship was destined to dock firstly at Southampton Water where the injured men would be unloaded to the Royal Victoria Hospital at Netley. The boat would then continue up to Southampton, where it would then be cleared of the other cargo. The boat suddenly shook as it vibrated, then strongly jolted forward, as the noise coming from the nearby engines, began to roar into the life. As the engines progressively got louder, it became difficult to continue any conversation, without shouting to be heard over the noise. The vibration of the boat could now be clearly felt through the floor, as both men now knew that the boat, was now in motion. Both Garvin and Francis for the first time during these past few days, began to feel a sense of relief, that they had at last now left France, and a satisfaction in the ease to which their passage to Dieppe had been undertaken.

The Stevedore had soon returned back to the room, with a plate full of fried bacon and half a loaf, to which all three men now devoured. For Garvin and Francis not used to warm cooked food, it wasn't long before both men were feeling tired, as they began to fall asleep regardless of the noise and heat being experienced within the small room, and much needed rest, before the remainder of their journey back to England. The Stevedore then left both men inside the room, whilst he continued with his other duties onboard the boat.

The journey from Dieppe across to Southampton Water was to take around five hours, although the boat was displaying the ensign of the 'Red Cross' to highlight as Hospital cargo, it would not be immune to possible 'U. Boat' attacks, whilst in the open English Channel. The vessel was unescorted in the open water of the mid-Channel. It would only be a matter of fortune, that there were no 'U. Boats' within the vicinity, or if they would acknowledge the 'Red Cross' ensign being displayed by the boat. The boat sailed unhindered across the English Channel, and was soon back into the safety of British controlled waters, where they were then within sight of the Isle of Wight, as the dawn began to appear over the eastern horizon. Garvin and Francis both woke feeling so refreshed from their all to brief sleep, and with the advantage of the boat crossing of the Channel being so smooth and calm. Both had decided it was too much of a risk to be seen on any of the upper decks, and the possibility of questioning by any Officer, so they chose to remain inside the cargo hold for the duration of the voyage. Toward the front of the cargo hold were two portholes located to either side of the hold, which enabled both men to view their outside surroundings in the early morning light. They could now see land on either sides of the boat, and could distinctly feel the boats vibration reduce, the Stevedore had returned to the hold, and told them, that they would be docking at Netley pier, in around twenty minutes time.

Now it was time to make another decision, should they make their escape and leave the boat at Netley, or continue up to Southampton, with the remainder of the cargo? Francis thought that Netley might have less Military personal in attendance, in comparison to the port of Southampton, given the level of logistics and Military hardware that were passing through the port. Garvin agreed with this, and it was decided by both to depart the boat at Netley. To minimise any suspicion, they would have to involve the assistance of carrying wounded Soldiers off the boat, and then hopefully disappearing through the Hospital grounds of Netley. The boat came to a halt and had now berthed against the pier of the Royal Victoria Hospital, as both made their way up toward the lower deck. They told the Stevedore they were to 'muck in' removing the troops, and would be back to continue the short journey up to Southampton.

What came next both shocked and deeply affected both men, and was beyond the comprehension of anything that they had seen in battle previously. It was now full light with the early morning sun shining into the large room located on the lower deck. Stretches were laid side by side in the room, each supporting an injured man. The smell overcame them both, as they entered into the room. Shattered men, of all shapes and sizes littered the floor, with injuries so hideous, they were often unrecognisable as human beings. Most were still alive, but they could see that some individuals, had not survived the journey. Garvin was emotionally overcome by this whole sight, and had to step back outside onto the deck, with his eyes now beginning to water, and was quickly followed outside by Francis.

"That's why I have to get away from this fucking war" as he spoke to Francis.

Garvin was quite a hard man, and Francis was so surprised to see him affected by his emotion at this sight, he had soon re-composed himself, as they returned back into the room. Both followed the Nursing Orderlies, by picking up and carrying a stretcher out of the room and onto the deck. A single gangplank had been lowered on to the pier, to which five Military Ambulances had been reversed toward the end of the pier. Each Ambulance could hold four stretchers under their canvass hood. They carried the stretcher of a young Soldier, who appeared to have lost his leg, he smiled at Francis as they carried him out of that room, and into the fresh morning air. Down the gangplank, as he was loaded onto the furthest Ambulance from the boat, within seconds the Ambulance was pulling away, and heading toward the giant building of the Royal Victoria Hospital which so dominated this part of the skyline. Garvin wanted to go now, whilst Francis considered getting more injured Soldiers off the boat, but as Garvin explained, this early unloading chaos was possibly their best time for them to disappear, as they were soon heading away from the boat, and walking along the wooden pier toward the shoreline. The Hospital grounds of the Royal Victoria were immense, as were reflected by the size of the vast building. They could even see that the Hospital had its own railway station, such was the scale of this facility. Both men calmly walked though the Hospital grounds, and upon reaching the open gates, were simply given a cursory nod by the Soldier who was stationed on guard duty.

Both men were so relieved they had made it this far, and were now back in England, as they walked briskly away from the Hospital gates. They followed a tree lined lane, which later transversed a single rail line, as the lane then followed the rail line in its direction toward Southampton. Rather than attempt to board a train at the Netley railway station, Garvin suggested they walk toward the next village, and to board the train there. Two miles along this lane, they had reached the village of Scholing, and entered into the empty waiting room of the railway station.

All trains from here were headed toward Southampton, located around five miles away from Scholing. Although they had avoided the port area of Southampton by alighting at Netley, they both knew that Southampton would still be a high risk destination. They assumed that once they were at Southampton Railway Station, there would be frequent trains to take them on to London. They had very little British money to use for food, but hoped that whilst still in their uniforms, this would enable them to free rail travel back toward Sheffield. A train had soon arrived at Scholing Railway Station heading in the direction of Southampton, as they both quickly left the waiting room, and climbed into the single carriage painted in the green livery, of the 'Southern Railway Company'. The conductor just looked over to the men, nodded, and said nothing, as he walked back toward the rear of the carriage, much to the relief of both. They were the only two passengers inside the carriage, and as they travelled along the rail line they could see that to the left of the train was Southampton Water, with several boats at anchor in the port, whilst rolling ploughed fields stretched away in the distance from the right hand side of the rail line. Gradually the surroundings were to become more urban, with houses and factories becoming more noticeable, as the train then crossed over a wide river, and into the city of Southampton. Once over the river, the train slowed to a halt at a railway station called St Denys, where Garvin had noticed a sign on the opposite platform, highlighting 'Trains to London.' Pulling Francis up with him, they both quickly alighted the train, before it continued on its destination to Southampton Railway Station.

Garvin then had to explain to Francis for his actions, and in his haste to leave the train, he now assumed that this was probably a much safer option for them both, rather than alighting at Southampton Railway Station, and the threat of being questioned by the Military Police. St Denys Railway Station was the first stop for trains travelling on the London line from Southampton, and only a small suburban station, situated adjacent to a coal yard and nearby gas plant. To their advantage, there were no Military in attendance at this small station.

Both men entered the small waiting room, hoping to remain out of sight until the London bound train would arrive. The waiting room had five other people who were sat quietly inside, and also waiting for the London bound train to arrive. A Soldier also heading for London, was sat alone in the corner of the waiting room. He immediately headed straight over toward both men, asking for a light to his cigarette, and attempting to develop a conversation with his two counterparts.

He was with the Middlesex regiment, and explained that he had been delayed from the rest of his unit over in France, where he had been forced to travel across to Southampton, whilst the remainder of his unit had all travelled back to London via Chatham, on the previous day. He seemed quite chatty to both men, he appeared to be a friendly and amicable sort of guy as most Londoners tended to be. The Middlesex regiment had been given a week's leave, before their embarkation to Egypt, and he was quite annoyed at already having missed a day's leave, and the inconvenience of having to travel through Southampton, back to London. Garvin then relayed to him a similar story, about both of them being on a forty-eight hour leave pass, and stated that they were to re-join the York's and Lancs regiment at Colchester. Them both being in Southampton to visit an injured comrade at the Royal Victoria Hospital, as there would be no way of either of them being able to travel back up to Sheffield, in that brief time. The Soldier agreed, and commented on what a set of 'complete bastards,' the Army were. Also sat in the waiting room was a young lady with a small child, who kept reminding all three men, about their coarse language in front of the child, to which they all duly apologised.

Following on from this brief conversation, the steam from the approaching train could now be seen over the rooftops of the adjacent houses, before it came into view, on its approach to St Denys Railway Station. The train slowed to a halt, as all the passengers hastily left the waiting room and made their way to board the train. The train was made up of five passenger carriages, again all painted in the green livery of the Southern Railway Company. More Soldiers and Sailors, could be seen through the windows of the carriages, as Francis then pulled open the door. They soon found an empty compartment, as all three men sat back, and settled into the high backed seats.

The Guards whistle then blew, as the train pulled forward, and very soon was travelling through the open and rolling hills of the Hampshire countryside. Both men now began to realise, that they were nearly 'home and dry,' and began to relax further, from their heightened state, relieved in the knowledge that they were now back in England and heading toward London. The Middlesex Soldier, then left the compartment, as he walked along the corridor to use the toilet that was situated between both carriages. He had left behind his backpack, as Garvin was soon quickly unfastening this, as the Soldier had left the compartment. Francis tried to stop Garvin, as he was not happy at Garvin at stealing anything from another Soldier. But it transcribed that Garvin was only after his Army identification card, always kept in the Army issued leather wallet. He soon found the card, and then swapped the card for his own identification card, as he fastened back the bag. He then passed the card over to Francis, to hide.

"What have you done that for?" asked Francis

"London, we have a lidget pass now, to get us into St Pancras" he replied to him.

"Can tha remember travelling through London, to France?" he asked him.

"Yes" Francis replied.

"Well, the obvious pick up point for deserters, who have made it back to England is London, and it will be crawling with Military Police outside the stations" he replied.

"But we only have that one card?' asked Francis

"Don't thee worry over that, ill get it out to thee, after I've got in" he replied.

What was so coincidental, was that as soon as the Middlesex Soldier had returned back to the carriage compartment, he was followed inside by the Train Conductor, who then asked all three men for their Army identification cards. There would be little chance that the conductor would realise that Francis and Garvin were both deserters, as he simply offered a cursory glance at each card, and then gave all three men a ticket each. Francis was now quite worried that the Middlesex Soldier might notice his different identification card. Garvin quickly struck up a conversation with the Middlesex Soldier at the very moment he was producing his card to the Conductor. This had the added effect of distracting him, and in the hope that he would not notice his card was now slightly different. He didn't notice, as all three men continued with their journey toward London. On their arrival at Waterloo Railway Station, both bid farewell to the Middlesex Soldier, as Francis and Garvin alighted the train. They passed over their tickets to the guard inside the exit booth, and quickly moved out of the station concourse toward the busy road outside They could now see that the entrance concourse to the platforms were thronged with Military Police, checking the details of all serviceman arriving at the station, for their departure.

Once outside Waterloo Railway Station, they crossed over the busy road, and decided to visit a pub further along the road, for a much needed drink. The pub was called 'The Blind Beggar,'as both men entered into the near empty saloon bar. They had about three shillings between them both, so a celebratory pint of English beer, was just what was needed, before the remainder of their journey. The Barman immediately poured two pints of bitter and passed them up onto the bar, holding up his hand, as to signal 'no charge.' As both men drank the pints immediately to which he duly obliged by pouring two more, to which this time, he asked for eight pence. Again both men, drank the pints down immediately, and duly ordered themselves two more, yet this time it was drank in a more relaxed manner, as they now engaged into conversation with the Barman. They asked him for directions to St Pancras Railway Station, as the Barman responded by highlighting to them the appropriate Underground Station, and the direction in which they should travel. They left the 'Blind Beggar,' but both were quite hesitant at the prospect of travelling on the Underground Railway, due to the number of Military Police, possibly be also on guard duty, as they had earlier experienced at Waterloo. They asked a passer by for directions to St Pancras, and again he pointed them in the direction of the Underground. They thanked him, but were soon heading in the opposite direction, toward the River Thames, and crossed over the Waterloo Bridge, and into central London. The constant noise of Tramcar, Omnibuses, and other horse drawn traffic, filled the crowded London streets. They had soon walked into The Strand, and passing by the Waldorf Hotel, they observed several well dressed ladies, and their gentleman companions, arriving at the hotel for some function, and yet this all seemed so oblivious, to the suffering and hardship that was being experienced by their fellow countrymen, over in Northern France.

Leaving the Strand, they then walked into Kingsway, where Francis noticed that a passing Tramcar had 'Euston,' highlighted onto its destination boards. The Tramcar was stood stationary waiting at a junction in the road, so they ran and had jumped onto the rear platform, as both men sat down on the lower deck. The Tramcar Conductor just acknowledged both of the uniformed men, with a cursory nod in their direction, as the Tramcar slowly pulled away from the junction.

What happened next was a shock to both men, as they were totally unprepared, when suddenly the Tramcar descended and disappeared from the street level, as it descended down a steep slope, and into an underground Tramway Station. Both men were quite apprehensive at this sudden development, and both began to panic at the thought of this being part of the Underground Railway system, and the strong possibility of Military Police being in attendance down here. Garvin was now considering jumping off the Tramcar, and running back up the track slope, to the street level above, but Francis held him back by the arm, highlighting that should the Military Police be down here, any action like this would raise further suspicion. The Tramcar pulled up to a halt, alongside an 'island platform,' where both the Driver and Conductor alighted, and disappeared into windowless brick built building, located toward the end of the short platform, and leaving all of the passengers sat waiting on the Tramcar. Much to the relief of both men was no one else was stood at the platform, and the fear of the Military Police, had soon subsided.

After around five minutes of waiting, a different Diver and Conductor, came out of the brick building, followed by the original Conductor and Driver, but both now dressed in their civilian clothes. The new Driver and Conductor climbed aboard, as the Tramcar now slowly moved forward. As they passed this brick building toward the end of the platform, Garvin had noticed that the door of the building had been left slightly open. The bright electric light shining from inside, highlighted a row of clothing and uniforms all hung up onto hangers, set against the back wall of the building. Garvin nudged Francis to highlight this, and told him they should get off at the next stop, and then go back down into the Underground Station. The Tramcar travelled along the underground trackbed for another three hundred yards, before climbing back up to the street level once more. As they both alighted the Tramcar at the next stop. Garvin explained to Francis, of his intention to acquire them both civilian clothing from this building on the platform, that would assist them on their journey back toward Sheffield.

"We walk back up this road, and we can go back down to that station on the stairs, we can wait on't platform until it's clear, and then sneak into that building, to get us some clothes" explained Garvin

"But we haven't enough money, to travel as civilians on the train, we still need uniforms, to pass" replied Francis.

"I know we get changed when we're near Sheffield, then blend in on our arrival, they'll be Military Police in Sheffield an all, that knows." replied Garvin.

Francis had come to trust Garvin immensely with his fate in this whole undertaking, had it not been for the strategic vision of Garvin in all of this, he wouldn't have got this far by himself. Garvin was such an opportunist, but he assessed every situation, in order to keep one step ahead. The final obstacle would be St

Pancras Railway Station, but both knew it would be 'plain sailing' once beyond St Pancras, and of their journey north.

They descended the stairs, and back into the underground Kingsway Tramway Station, a Tramcar was sat waiting at the platform, as once more the Conductor and Driver had alighted, to possibly change shifts. In the gloom of the island platform, Both men sat on one of the many benches near to the brick building, to be assumed that they were simply waiting for a Tramcar travelling in the opposite direction. Replicating the earlier Tramcar journey, four people then emerged from the brick building, Driver, Conductor, and two civilians. This time all four boarded the waiting tramcar, as it slowly pulled away. The platform was now deserted, as Garvin moved toward the brick building, as he slowly pushed at the open the door, there was no one inside. He looked up and down the clothing, and passed Francis two cotton shirts which he quickly stuffed into inside his overcoat pocket. Garvin then rolled up and placed two pairs of trousers, obtained from two civilian suits, that were hung up, into his own overcoat. He then took off his own overcoat, and put on one of the suit jackets, and beckoned Francis to do the same. They then put back on their overcoats and to hide the jackets from view. Francis's suit jacket proved to be quite tight, given his size, but they had no time to select, as everything would have to suffice in these circumstances.

The rumble of a Tramcar could now be clearly heard descending the slope and was approaching the platform, as both men calmly walked out of the building, and stood toward the edge of the platform. Both climbed onboard the Tramcar, but on this occasion the Tramcar pulled away as soon as they were seated. The Conductor once more, just nodded in the direction of both men, as they sat together on the lower deck. The Tramcar was soon climbing back up to the street level, as it continued along the Kingsway toward Euston Station.

Garvin had travelled to France through Euston Railway Station earlier that year, and he knew that St Pancras Railway Station, was quite near to the Tramcar's destination of Euston Railway Station. Now their greatest challenge would be getting past the Military Police on the station concourse of St Pancras. Francis had every confidence that Garvin would get them both beyond St Pancras, or would Garvin now simply use the stolen Army identification card for his own purpose, and to leave Francis stranded in London. He had no choice but to let Garvin go ahead with the undertaking in the hope he could be trusted to get the card back out to him somehow, once he was past the Military Police. In all his undertakings previously with Garvin, he had realised that he was an honourable man, and he had every confidence the stolen identification card would be passed back to him, by some method.

The red brick gothic building with its large ornate spires, and the imposing clock tower of the St Pancras Hotel and Station, were such an impressive sight to any man approaching from the Euston Road, but to Garvin and Francis, this would be their final barrier to overcome, as their freedom lay beyond this building. They had come this far, and to fail at this last hurdle, would probably lead to them both returning back to the trenches, or possible death by a firing squad. Garvin always the more confident of the pair, was quite upbeat as to what lay beyond that station concourse, Francis again naturally apprehensive, at the whole undertaking. All they needed now was a way of getting the stolen Army identification card back out to Francis, once Garvin was inside the station.

Entering the station firstly had to be undertaken by Garvin, he would be the one to notice any lax security, or of possible entrances onto the platform, once he was beyond the concourse. Looking at the pedestrian and vehicular activity of traffic on the station approach, it was to be assumed that St Pancras would be quite busy inside, as this would be to the advantage of both fugitives. Immediately located across the Euston Road from the station, were two cast iron post boxes, placed to separate the different classification of mail. They realised this would be a suitable and identifiable vantage point for Francis to wait, but firstly they would take a walk around the station perimeter, just to check on the security and of possible access points. As they both expected, the rear of the station was secure, with no breaks in the security fencing, to allow them access to the platform. It soon became the reality that they had no choice but to pass through the station concourse, and to show the identity card to the Military Police. Garvin needed to assess the situation once he was inside the station, and as to how he could then get Francis inside. There was no other choice than for Garvin to enter the station, as he told Francis to wait by the post boxes situated across the Euston Road, and he would get the identification card out to him in due course.

Garvin slowly walked up the station approach, and past the St Pancras Hotel. He entered the passenger entrance, he was already warm and sweating due to the suit jacket being worn underneath his thick Army overcoat, as his anxious fear also contributed to this state. He tried to compose himself, and to wipe away the sweat from underneath his cap. As he neared the station concourse, he could see it was already full with both civilians, and other such Military personal. A queue of Soldiers, many still covered in the dried mud and other such debris from their time in France and travelling on their way home on leave, were waiting to pass through the line of Military Police, at the platform gate. Garvin noticed that the identification cards were all being individually checked and scrutinised by the Military

Police, and were not being waved through as could often happen with large crowds. He queued for around fifteen minutes, as the line of Soldiers slowly passed through to the checkpoint. As he neared toward the front of the queue, he noticed that the Military Police were also asking names, and to what regiment each man belonged to. The stolen identification card, had belonged to a Harold Lambert of the Middlesex rifles, yet Garvin was still wearing the insignia of the West Riding regiment, on both his uniform and his cap. He was by now physically shaking, and there was nothing he could do to get out of this, without raising any suspicion from the Military Police. He slowly approached the Military Police Officer, as he held out his Identification card, in a feeble attempt to disguise the regiment detail, he placed his thumb over the Middlesex insignia. The Military Police Officer then looked directly at the card, at which point Garvin coughed, and dropped the card onto the floor, apologising to the Officer. He crouched down to pick up the card and as he stood back up, he was immediately waved through to the platform gates by the Officer.

To his immense relief he was through, and was now able to continue on his journey to Sheffield, he sat down on a platform bench, just relieved he had made it through this final hurdle. His shivering and his sweating now slowly began to recede, as he sat staring at the stationary trains, waiting along the other platforms. He could see back through the open station approach that it was now nightfall, and nearly dark outside. As he surveyed the scene, and the options of getting Francis inside, and how to get the stolen identification card to him on the outside. He scoured the station, with the possibility of accessing the Hotel from the platform, and attempting to drop the card out of the window, but how could he discreetly attract the attention of Francis, from across the busy Euston Road.

He sat with a deep realisation that it might now be impossible to get Francis inside the station, and have to abandon him in London. A Guard then walked up to a stationary train placed down a blackboard as he began to chalk up the destination stations of the Train, which was about to depart. Bedford, Leicester, Derby, Ilkeston, Chesterfield, Sheffield, Barnsley, Wakefield and Leeds were the highlighted destinations.

Several Soldiers had now begun to gather in the vicinity of the train, as Garvin desperately tried to think of a solution for Francis. Passing through the Soldiers was a ragged looking paperboy, handing out free copies of the Daily Mirror to the waiting troops. He approached Garvin.

"Free daily, Soldier?" he asked Garvin.

"Yes son, and do you want to earn sum money, and do me an errand?" replied Garvin

"What like?" he asked.

"My mate is waiting for me outside, he is stood at the post box across the road, he's forgotten his card, and he can't get on this train without it. Will yer do us a favour and tek it him, I'll watch your papers" said Garvin.

"How much" he asked him, as Garvin reached into his pockets and realised Francis had all their money.

"He'll pay thi outside" replied Garvin.

"Oh yeah, think I was born yesterday" replied the youth.

"Alreight what about me cap then," as he offered his Army cap to the youth.

He took the cap, and tried it on, whilst Garvin passed him the card.

"What's he look like?" asked the youth.

"Big bloke stood at the post boxes, they call him William" replied Garvin

As soon as he had offered this, the youth passed Garvin his bag of newspapers, and ran along the platform toward the station concourse, whilst wearing Garvin's Army cap. He ran straight across the concourse, past the Military Police to the outside of the Station. He continued running along the station approach, as he quickly crossed the road, by dodging the passing traffic. As he approached both post boxes, he could see a large man in uniform stood by them.

"You William mate?" he asked Francis.

"A Soldier inside the station, asked me to pass you this" as he passed Francis the identification card.

The youth then ran back across the busy road, and back into the Station, where he soon found Garvin still sat with his newspapers, he nodded at Garvin, picked up the papers, and continued to pass them out to the waiting Soldiers. Several Soldiers were now beginning to board the Sheffield bound train, and the platform was soon emptying from the earlier bustle. Garvin on the continual lookout for Francis, then moved toward the platform entrance gate.

Francis had crossed the Euston Road, and walked up the Station approach, and onto the Station concourse, similar to Garvin's entrance only forty minutes earlier, and joined the queue to the Military Police checkpoint, where he stood patiently in line. Garvin was hoping that Francis would have recited the card details, and to remember the Middlesex Rifles as he approached the Military Police. Garvin watched the proceedings from the safety of the platform, as Francis then held out the card to the Officer. In what seemed to be an eternity, he could see the Military Police Officer speak to Francis then waved him through. The relief on Francis's face was immense, as he calmly walked through the gate to the platform entrance, as both men looked at each other both sporting a slight grin.

They had soon boarded the Sheffield bound train, and within five minutes it was slowly pulling forward, much to the relief of both men. The young paperboy could be seen out of the carriage window and was still wearing Garvin's cap, he recognised Garvin through the window as they slowly passed on the train, as he stood to attention and saluted Garvin. Both men sat back, and now relaxed as all that was left for them to do was to change into they're newly acquired civilian clothing, once they were beyond Chesterfield, as the train now headed toward Sheffield.

Chapter 6 - Return to Sheffield.

Both men disembarked from the train at the Sheffield Midland railway station, in the cold of the early morning air. The steam from the train being further highlighted, as the locomotive stood waiting for the guard to signal, and continue its journey to Leeds. The station platforms were all deserted at this early hour, and only the activity of freight being unloaded from another train broke the silence. They could now see the ramshackle houses of the Park district, clinging onto the hillside above the station as all seemed to be looking downward onto the station platforms given their close proximity. Garvin knew of a quiet route out of the station, and was located toward the far end of the platform. This would be a single iron gate used only by the track maintenance crews. Garvin knew that the gate was usually kept unlocked, as it opened up behind some iron steps, that ascended to a footbridge which transversed the rail lines, and linked up South Street with Turner Street. They slipped through the narrow iron gate, as they made their way across the footbridge, and both men were soon within the familiar haunts of Garvin, and the notorious Park district. Francis would again be so reliant upon Garvin, and of this unfamiliar place of Sheffield. The narrow alleyways, and courts above South Street, enabled both fugitive's some relief from the possibility of being sighted of either the Military or civilian Police within the area, as both knew they were not yet quite safe, from this threat.

Rather than go immediately to his own house on School Lane, Garvin made straight for the house of George Wheyhill a close friend, and also member of the Park Brigade in which to seek sanctuary, from the early morning cold. Wheyhill was not awake at this early hour, as they arrived at his house, as his wife was suddenly awakened by the throwing of small stones, up toward the bedroom window by Garvin. The frame of the window was jammed shut, but she immediately recognised Garvin, through the window as she woke her husband. Wheyhill then rushed downstairs, as he immediately let both men into the kitchen scullery, and out of the cold morning air.

"What the bleeding hell are tha doing back here, and how come tha not in uniform?" asked Wheyhill.

"As tha got owt to eat, for us both?" replied Garvin.

"I'll get her to do both some bread and jam, but what tha doing back here?"

"This is William, William Francis from Boston, we've done one, pissed off with it all, and need to keep an eye on things back here" he replied.

Wheyhill's wife was now dressed, as she came into the scullery, and proceeded to light the gas ring, she cut the men some bread from a loaf, to which Garvin grabbed from her, and ate immediately, before she had chance to even spread the jam. Garvin then continued with the conversation, as he chewed, with his mouth still full of bread.

"We've come ere first, hoping tha could get us somewhere to sleep, I can't go to our house, they will be watching that like a sparrow hawk."

"Where's yer uniform?" asked Wheyhill

"We nicked these suits off two guys in London, and have travelled up by train, I have a little money, if that's of any use" replied Francis.

"Keep hold of that, I'll nip out in a bit, and see what a can do, Agnes get the fire lit and keep these two warm"

The house was typical of a three story court house, and already showing signs of neglect, and a run-down appearance, so typical of many houses within this district. As the early morning progressed Wheyhill's three children were all quickly given a slice of bread each, and dispatched outside, being warned not to speak of these visitors to anyone. Wheyhill left the house about an hour later, firstly up to 'Sky Edge,' just to check on matters and all was in order for the commencement of betting. Then made his way down toward the Sheffield Market, located just off Broad Lane and near to the bottom of Duke Street. He was familiar with a number of traders at the market who he knew that he could trust, to help Garvin. Jimmy Dyson was such a man, and he held a fruit and veg stall in the market, as he also rented a lock up in the small arches of the Victoria station approach, just across from the markets, located on Furnival Road. Jimmy agreed that both men could sleep in the lock up, until something more permanent could be found for them both.

Both men then waited inside the house of Wheyhill until nightfall later that day, and along with Wheyhill carefully made their way down toward Furnival Road and the lock up. Very few people were in the area, as the three men took a carefully planned route to avoid detection through the back streets of the Park district. All walked down toward Blast Lane, around the rear of the Corn Exchange, and Canal Basin until they reached the large wooden doors of Dyson's lock up in the arches, the keys were then passed over to Garvin by Wheyhill.

The lock up arch, had a stone frontage, and brick lined inside, with a blank brick wall located at the rear, of the arch, it was built to support the road above, which was the main approach toward the Victoria railway station. The arch was secured from Furnival Road by two large wooden doors, and inside were two handcarts and several crates of raw vegetables. Both men were soon at home in the arch as Wheyhill had also brought along three candles, a box of matches, and with the large amount of straw on the lock up floor, was soon gathered to make beds for both men. Wheyhill then left the men to settle down for the night, promising to return on the following morning.

At around nine o'clock that night there was a loud knock on the door of the lock up. Both men ignored the knocking which soon increased in its intensity, as someone knew they were both inside the arch. Garvin was so hesitant about answering, but Francis realised that no one knew him in Sheffield, so he cautiously moved toward the door, whilst Garvin hid. He could see through the gap in the door frame that is was the outline of a lady, as he unlocked one of the doors, and slightly pushed the door forward. It was a middle aged lady all dressed in black wearing spectacles, carrying a covered basket, and a jug.

"I've come for our Samuel, is he in here?" she asked abruptly.

"Me mam!" came a loud response from Garvin now hiding toward the rear of the arch. She had brought some bread, cheese, and a jug of beer. She stepped inside the arch, as Francis closed the door directly behind her.

"What tha done this for, they'll be looking for thi now" she spoke directly at Garvin.

"Sod em, too much to do ere, and I need to earn us some money. This is William, he's from Boston, he's come from France with mi, nowt over there for us" said Garvin.

"Hello Mrs Garvin, nice to meet you," holding out his hand. She didn't respond or even acknowledge this, as she looked directly toward Garvin.

"George has gone over to the Crofts to see if there a lodging house with a room for you, they are all full of Irish at the moment working in't factories, but am sure he will get yer summat."

"He's a good lad George, am sure he will, anyway thas best get thi sen back, or coppers will be watching yer, I'll be in touch soon" as he bid her goodbye.

At that point Francis then opened the large door for her, as she made her way directly across the Furnival Road. Mrs Garvin quickly left Furnival Road, so as to avoid any further suspicion by the Police, as she made her way back toward her house on School Lane. Both men had soon finished off the food and beer, and began to settle down onto the straw beds, for remainder of the night. They were soon wakened by the scuttling and continual scratching of rats located somewhere in the arch. This didn't bother them too much, as they had encountered many rats whilst in the trenches, but within the confines of the arch, this further amplified their presence. It was not to be unexpected in an archway with vegetable remnants scattered, and several canal side warehouses situated directly across Furnival Road, but the constant noise of shuffling and squealing, kept both men awake for most of that night. The following morning Wheyhill, had brought breakfast and some money for both fugitives, he also brought along a flat cap for Garvin to wear. This would enable him some form of disguise, and able to walk the streets, without the fear of being instantly recognised by the Police or any other associates.

Garvin pulled the cap tightly over his head, as they proceeded to a public house known as the Vaults near to the market, here they both drank a couple of pints, made use of the toilets and a freshen up and wash, in the back room of the pub. Garvin was keen to show Francis the sights of this part of Sheffield and the market, where they were soon easily lost in the large crowds, of the area. Around two o clock Garvin decided it was time to show Francis the gambling operation up at 'Sky Edge'. Although they were both cautious as not to be seen in the Park district until Police enquiries had settled down, they were able to board an Intake bound tramcar up City Road toward 'Sky Edge,' and to access the area along from Manor Lane, thus avoiding walking within the Park district.

They then made their way up to the High Street via the thirty steps, to Fitzalan Square and called into the Bell Hotel for another quick drink, before their short wait on High Street for several until the blue and cream double decked Intake bound tramcar had arrived. Both men jumped on board the tramcar, and sat down on the lower deck, as the tramcar quickly pulled away. Garvin was soon pointing out to Francis several highlights as the tramcar climbed on its journey out of the city, along Duke Street and the City Road, toward Manor Lane.

The tramcar conductor then rang the bell for the tramcar to halt, directly at the bottom of Manor Lane. as both men then alighted. Garvin turned toward Francis and asked him "well what's tha think? this is the nicer bit just up here, and then there's a path to the edge through them trees" as he pointed up the hill of Manor Lane.

Francis replied "It's bleeding hilly, it had better be worth it" as they climbed the hill from City Road along Manor Lane, toward 'Sky Edge.'

Toward the top of the hill, they proceeded along an unmade path, and through some woodland, where they encountered a single youth, asking them where they were going. The youth was around fourteen years old, and oblivious, as to who Sam Garvin was. Garvin then grabbed the youth by the lapels of his jacket, and flung him into some bushes to the side of the pathway.

"Don't thee ever ask who I am, again, and why are tha stood ere, when we are nearly at the rings. Tha should be at the entrance to these woods, and not stood here, so get thi sen up there!" as Garvin abruptly addressed the youth.

Quickly the youth picked himself up, and began to run toward the entrance of the wood, it was obvious he was a 'Pikey' the paid look outs posted at various points around 'Sky Edge.' As Garvin had pointed out, he would be of little use to warn the others, in the place where he was stood.

"See! things have slipped, let's see what else we'll bleeding find" said Garvin.

As both men approached toward the gambling rings, they could see it was quite full, with around seventy men, stood around the four gambling rings. Garvin was quickly greeted by many of the men, as if he was a long lost family relative, all were pleased to see him back at 'Sky Edge.' The gambling rings were mostly used for a game known as 'pitch and toss', where men would gamble on the outcome of three coins being tossed into the ring, and of their head or tail position, upon landing. Garvin went on to explain to Francis that the gambling ring was busy due to the afternoon shift change, that had taken place in many of the nearby steel and engineering works of the city. Many of the morning workers were now at the ring, and were keen to earn an extra income, to supplement their wages.

All was quiet, until a large and irate Irishman, accused the 'bookmaker' of cheating on him, as the winning odds were not the same, as at the time he had placed the bet. He quickly squared up to the 'bookmaker' and asked for his money back.

Another Irishman who Francis, could see was one of the Park men, tried to reason with the irate Irishman, who was adamant that he wanted his money back. The Park man then told him "no money given back,"and produced a poker, from the inside of his jacket lining threatening to use it on the man. The stature of the irate Irishman much exceeded that of the Park man, but he was fearless in confronting him.

The Irishman then tried to grab the poker from him, but the Park man was just too fast, to which several successive blows form the poker were dealt toward both his arms and torso. The Irishman grabbed at his arm, and in such severe pain from the poker blow, as the Park man then punched him directly in the face. Soon the Park man began to reign several fierce blows toward the Irishman, who was soon knocked onto the floor, his face and hair now becoming a mass of blood. Francis just stood back and watched the proceedings, as this was up until now a fair fight and had no doubt this was the way that justice was dealt with by the Park men. As the Irishman then lay on the floor, five other men, including Garvin stood all stood around him, and began kicking him with force. Francis was quite took back at this action, and such an unfair fight, but realised it was in his best interests to stay out of the proceedings. Garvin then knelt down at the Irishman's side, he lifted his head up by his hair and spoke.

"If you're gonna loose, be fuckin man enough to tek it, now fuck off". Dropping the man's head back to the ground.

The gambling had soon resumed, from this unexpected interruption, and nobody even noticed when the Irishman picked himself up, and slipped off on his way back toward town. Garvin introduced Francis to the man who had earlier confronted the Irishman, as George Mooney, known by Garvin simply as 'Irish George.'

Mooney was quite older than the other Park men, being about thirty years old, and had a reputation as both a hard man, and of being fearless in any fight. He had been associated with Garvin and the Park men for a number of years, although he didn't actually live in the Park district, but was always seen by Garvin as being very loyal and trustworthy. Following Garvin's conscription into the Army, Mooney had been tasked along with George Wheyhill, of keeping the gambling ring active during the lucrative war years. Excused active service due to him being of Irish descent, George Mooney had taken a munitions job as a result of this, but he soon grew bored of the relentless workload, so he held down a part time job as a window cleaner working in the city centre. The window cleaning work being undertaken during the early mornings, as he further supplemented his earnings at 'Sky Edge' during the afternoons. The gambling ring was becoming quite well known and had now began to attract men from outside of Sheffield, such was the reputation, and the relative isolation of 'Sky Edge.' Garvin had been very keen to hear of all this, whilst he was away, and had no doubt that the monies now being taken,by the Park men had increased significantly. Although Garvin had known Mooney for a number of years, and had come to trust him, there was something that had earlier been highlighted by Wheyhill, which had given Garvin some suspicion around Mooney, and of the operation whilst he had been away in France.

Soon the men were joined by George Wheyhill, who told Garvin, that a lodging room had been found for them both at a house just off Scotland Street, in the notorious West Bar area of town.

"We will go back with 'Irish George,' to his house on Trinity Street, and let him warn off the Paddy's in the area first, before we go up to the lodging house" replied Garvin.

Around four o clock the gambling had ceased for the day, as the men dispersed along the many pathways leading away from 'Sky Edge,' many still betting with each other, on such trivial challenges they noticed, as they returned back to work, or home.

Garvin, Francis, and Mooney then left via Manor Lane, and caught the Intake tramcar back into the city centre. Mooney lived on Trinity Street located just off West Bar, located to the North side of the city centre. Once they had alighted the tramcar all three men quickly walked down Snig Hill toward West Bar, all were quite inconspicuous amongst the busy Sheffield streets of the late afternoon. Garvin was quite well known throughout the city, and even with this location being the opposite side of the city to the Park district, there was every possibility he might be recognised by the authorities. Both Garvin and Francis hadn't shaved for a number of days, so both still looked quite disheveled, with Garvin in his flat cap and worn tightly over his head to hide his face, and not as easily recognisable from his usual smart appearance.

All three men then went straight to Mooney's house in Trinity Street, and were soon made to feel at home by Mooney's wife, where they sat drinking hot tea, surrounded by Mooney's young children, in the parlour, of his house. Mooney firstly went over to the lodging house, and to warn the residents of the secrecy as to the identities of their new residents. As he then proceeded to the St Vincent's Catholic Men's Club at Croft House to relay to key members of the Irish community, for their co-operation with regard to housing these fugitives in West Bar. Garvin was also well known to many in the Irish community, who had often frequented 'Sky Edge.' It would not be in their interest to notify Garvin to the authorities, as many recalled they had always been treat fairly by Garvin in the past, and had no argument or score, to settle with him. As Francis was unknown to any of them, this was not considered to be an issue for the community. Mooney was respected and well known throughout the Irish community in Sheffield, no one would dare to cross Mooney, without consequences. The mistrust of the Irish community toward the authorities meant that there would be little chance of the whereabouts of Garvin or Francis being alerted toward them.

Mooney returned back to his house, and then escorted both men up to the lodging house. If members of the community kept to their word, there was no reason why both men could not remain hidden here for some time. This was an area well away from the Park district, where both the Military and Sheffield City Police, would not assume that Garvin would be heading. Because of the notoriety of the area around Scotland Street and West Bar, the Police were always cautious as to venture into this area. Less than half a mile from the city centre, this was definitely a hostile, and closed ghetto, to anyone who was brave enough to venture into. Off limits to many townsfolk, and a lack of trust to both the authorities and Police by the predominant Irish community, both Garvin and Francis would be quite safe staying here, until matters had quietened down.

The lodging house was a typical three story court house of the area, in much disrepair with broken windows, and approached through a cinder laid, court yard. Four other similar houses looked over the court, and the number 3Ct was painted crudely onto the flaking paintwork of the door. Four small children, accompanied by a dog were at play in the dirty cinder of the court, with four privies located into the corner of the court. No sunlight was emitted into the court, due to the large brick gabled end, of what looked like the outside of an adjacent factory unit, towering over the court houses. The sound of a forge and the hammering of metal could be clearly heard coming from the inside of the factory, to which the whole court vibrated with each hammer blow.

Mooney banged onto the door of 3Ct, as an elderly Irish guy answered and simply nodded for all three to enter the house. Once inside the small scullery, the warmth from the range could be clearly felt, and so different to the cold air outside. What was so noticeable was the constant vibration felt within the house, and the rattling of furniture, due to the regular hammer blows, coming from the factory toward the end of the court. This could clearly be felt through the bare clay floor of the downstairs room. Aside from the range, the only other noticeable piece of furniture inside this room, was an old oak table and five differing chairs, newspapers covered the table, as spilled traces of dried food could be seen on the newspapers. The room had a single sash window and a door leading outside to the court, with dirty patterned wallpaper and a gas mantle. To the rear of the room was another internal door, which to a staircase, and turned immediately right and over an alcove area, which was curtained off from the main room.

A voice could then be heard from behind that curtain, where in a strong Irish accent everyone was told to "Shut the fuck up, whilst I trying to get some sleep."

"You'se go shut yourself up" repeated the house owner in response to the man, as all four men climbed the stairs, up to the room to be let. There were two other rooms in the house, the first floor room as used by the owner, and another two lodgers, whilst Garvin and Francis had been given the attic room on the second floor of the house. As they climbed the steep stairs, a door at the top opened into the attic, where two beds were situated, placed at right angles to each other. This room was quite light in comparison to the other rooms of the house, and a skylight window in the roof gave sufficient light. This was certainly not the Ritz, but was so much an improvement, of the rat infested lock up on Furnival Road as was used on the previous night.

The guy who owned the house was possibly in his sixties and called Michael, he explained there were four other lodgers staying in the house, the rent was two shillings a week per man, and payable on a Friday. He told them, he had worked for many years as a railway navvy, and now being too old to work in such a role. All of the house residents were out at work, and the guy downstairs was on the night shift, later in the day. As they left the lodging house all three men, then proceeded back to Mooney's house, on Trinity Street where his wife had prepared them all some food.

As nightfall began to fall, and the daily bustle and activity outside of Trinity Street reduced, as all three men ventured out, and made their way up toward Scotland Street, where the many pubs would provide a safe refuge for both men before they went back to the lodging house. The pubs of Scotland Street usually frequented by working Irishmen, and many were quite rough establishments. Mooney bid them both a farewell and left them both outside the Queens Hotel, to which they both entered.

It wouldn't be long before a cursory wrong glance, had attracted attention to both fugitives, and soon Francis was being challenged to a fight outside in the street, by an over enthusiastic local. Francis duly obliged, and was soon back inside the pub after about five minutes, hitting the young pretender with a blow, that knocked him halfway across the cobbles of Scotland Street. The guy then suddenly realising his senses, ran off down Scotland Street, and much to the amusement of passing bystanders. Garvin remained seated inside the pub, given the size and strength of Francis he simply knew this would be the obvious outcome.

Garvin smiled at Francis as he re-entered the pub, as things soon returned back to normal. Around nine thirty the same guy who had run off earlier, now appeared back inside the pub and challenged Francis to another fight outside, and in his own words a fairer fight. Francis felt he was being humiliated by this guy, and he quickly followed him outside to take up the challenge, as he left the pub door, he was hit from behind by another man, who was already waiting, in the side passage of the pub. As he hit the floor another two men, quickly jumped onto Francis, and were quick to lay their boots and fists into his torso. He laid in agony on the pavement, reeling from the blows, whilst the young guy to whom he had, the earlier altercation, now hit him about his torso with a poker, which had been concealed on the inside of his jacket.

Francis desperately trying to get up, and back onto his feet, his left hand was stamped upon, but this time Garvin was stood directly behind the guy, who had administered this action. Garvin pulled out a poker from the inside of his jacket, and directly hit the guy, who then suddenly dropped toward the floor, and was out cold. Garvin then squared up to the other man, as he moved his arm in a swift movement, as the guy immediately fell to the floor, and was reeling about in agony, on the cobbles of Scotland Street, with his face covered by his hands. Blood could now be seen streaming though his hands, and it was obvious now, this guy had been slashed by Garvin. Upon seeing this, the other two guys just froze in fear, dropped the poker as used earlier on Francis, and ran off down Scotland Street toward Meadow Street. Francis managed to now climb to his feet, as both then decided to make their way back toward the lodging house, as he was helped by Garvin.

Back at the lodging house Garvin filled the face bowl with clean water from the outside pump, and helped to bathe Francis's wounds, with a towel, as both men soon retired to their beds. George Mooney arrived about eight o clock, on the following morning, and had already heard about the incident in Scotland Street, from the previous night. The guy who had been slashed, had to attend the Infirmary, and had received numerous stitches along the wound to his face. Garvin was quick to point out that they had started it, and asked if the guy had recognised who had done it. Mooney responded that the guy was a known trouble maker, and well known to the Police, and that they wouldn't take his statement seriously. None of them had realised it was Sam Garvin who was involved, but just some southern sounding English guy. Francis began to realise that fights on the streets of Sheffield were not like the fair fights he had ever been involved in, the use of weapons and other such was a common place practice, as was the uneven numbers of opponents.

It was still quite risky for Francis and Garvin to be seen up at 'Sky Edge' so both were content to spend most of the day at the billiards hall, located at the top end of Cambridge Street. Francis was still in a great amount of pain as he tried to take shots, from the previous days incident, but this soon subsided as the day progressed, and as they then both visited the cinema. They had arranged to meet Wheyhill and Mooney back in the Barley Corn Hotel, on Cambridge Street, to discuss the day's activities and for Garvin to be paid out his share. He was passed fifteen pounds, to which he immediately passed Francis five pounds, and saying to the others "My protector from the Paddy's."

This daily routine of living at the lodging house, billiards, and the cinema, lasted for about two weeks, it was soon noticeable that Garvin, wanted to be back in the Park district, amongst the pubs, clubs, and the gambling ring, where he generated so much respect. For Garvin having to live at the opposite side of the city felt so alien to him, and well away from his regular haunts.

Garvin actually went and met up with his own mother at the Adelphi Hotel for afternoon tea on one day, such was his desire to catch up with knowledge around the family, and following from his all too brief encounter with his mother at the lock up, on that first night back in Sheffield. She told him the Police had attended his house and undertaken searches on three occasions since his desertion from the Army, as he realised that Park might just be too risky, for the next few weeks at least.

The Great War was now making advances, and the Allies had at last made significant advances against the Germans, and in his own wisdom he contemplated that they might just forget about him and Francis, once the war was over. With so many men of active service age in Sheffield at this time, that were employed in the reserve occupations, both were able to blend in to the everyday surroundings of the city, with less chance of detection. Only certain 'eagle eyed' Police Officers, or the close associates of Garvin, were able to recognise him. With his flat cap placed tightly over his head, and his newly grown beard, Garvin looked so different from his usual smart and clean shaven appearance. To move back over to Park would be so risky for Garvin, although Francis would be able to pass unasumed with no problem. But his desire became so strong, and very soon a room was found for him to stay with George Wheyhill, although Wheyhill was considered to be a close associate, the search for Garvin was now beginning to reduce, as the Police considered he was possibly not even in Sheffield, as nothing had been seen of him, or any information had been passed regarding his whereabouts.

There would be no room for Francis to stay at Wheyhill's, house, so it was agreed that he would remain at the lodging house, but was able to travel freely between West Bar, and the Park district.

Garvin had soon moved into Wheyhill's house, as this arrangement then lasted for about three days, until he moved in with a young widow he had known from the area, called Mary Parkin. She lived with her two small children in a cottage located on Bard Street, her husband had been killed in a steelworks accident just before the Great War. Bard Street was at the lower side of the Park district, and quite near to the city centre. It was always quite a busy area, with the nearby Park Cinema, and the street led directly onto Broad Street, with direct access to the market and city centre.

Garvin so trusted Francis, and as no one knew him in Sheffield, and he wanted him to be his presence up at 'Sky Edge' on a daily basis to oversee matters. He wanted him to ensure that his share was forthcoming, as he didn't trust George Mooney anymore. If some of the stories he had already heard from Wheyhill about Mooney taking more of his share, were to be believed, he needed to know this. He told Francis as to how he wanted him to observe what was happening, and that he would only visit 'Sky Edge' on certain days for fear of him being recognised and apprehended by the Police. As the 'Great War' was possibly now in its later stages, the available money to many men of the city, could soon reduce, as the last few lucrative war years were coming to a close.

Garvin would often be known to many people as a thug, and a much self-centred man, yet underneath his exterior he was also quite a shrewd character, and always fully aware of what was happening all around him. The respect he afforded in the Park district was looked upon in envy, by some of the others within his group, and especially George Mooney, as he had built up this reputation, by being a such a ruthless individual. From his early days of stealing scrap metal and burglary, he built up a reputation, of shrewd planning and of quickly dealing with anyone who had crossed him. The control of 'Sky Edge' by the Park men, was a major coup, and building upon this lucrative business, from the bookmaker who had originally began the illegal operation. As leader of the group Garvin always carried an air of superiority, and this being cemented by his ruthless reputation, in quickly dealing with those who crossed him, and disappearing at the right time. Many folk of the Park district would cross the street at his approach, simply in fear as if he looked at them in the wrong way, pubs would quieten as he entered, and he was usually the recipient of free beer, and other such commodities in the pubs, and shops of the area. His fear was such, that he had the confidence that no one living in the Park district, would even dare notify the authorities of his return, but he just wanted to keep a low profile at this time, until the war was over.

Garvin trusted Francis, possibly down to the fact of what they had both been through together in France. Francis also coming from outside of town, he was still unknown to the others as he realised that Francis would have no particular allegiance, except to Garvin. He would pay for his lodgings in West Bar, and was also to give him ten shillings a week, to be his 'eyes and ears' up at 'Sky Edge.' This also meant Francis was now able to send money back to his mother in Sibsey Northlands, for the first time since his desertion from the Army. It was also common knowledge that Garvin could also be a very generous man, as Francis was to learn from the others, that it was wise to stay on the right side of him.

Francis attended Sky Edge at eight o clock on the following day, as men were beginning to arrive straight from their work on the night shift. The weather was damp, as rain fell over the city, and it was doubtful that any gambling would be going ahead on that morning. Soon George Mooney had arrived followed by another

Park man Frank Kidnew, and six other youths who were to be posted as 'Pikeys' for the remainder of that day. As the tossing rings were still wet, and were quite prone to difficulties for the pitch of the 'ring tossers' to ensure favourable conditions for this skill. To ensure some form of gambling could take place whilst it was still raining Mooney decided, that the six youths would fight each other for the four 'Pikey' look out places being on offer that day, with the three losers then fighting out for the fourth place. This soon proved to be a popular alternative for the men, so keen to bet their money. The odds being placed against each of the youths, based upon size and physique, as the series of three fights began. Quite soon only four victorious youths bloodied and bruised, as a result of the fights were allocated to the four 'Pikey' positions for that day, as the other two both injured were then ordered away from 'Sky Edge.'

What Francis did notice, was that during the third fight the odds were altered considerably against the winner. Only one punter had noticed this, as he immediately challenged Mooney during the pay out. Mooney was quick to make comment, that the rain had washed and possibly smudged the chalk, on the board, whilst the fight was taking place, and that these were the original odds that were chalked, and the guy was mistaken. The guy had clearly won more, but he had believed Mooney's explanation, upon collecting his reduced winnings. Francis had also noticed this, and that the guy was possibly due another two shillings as a result of this win. He quickly counted up around twelve other men, who had also won bets on this fight. Although this particular punters win was showing as two shillings down, if this was replicated with another twelve winners, at differing values, this would be quite a rip off being undertaken by Mooney.

Francis believed that Mooney hadn't yet considered as to why Garvin had placed him at 'Sky Edge,' and assumed that Mooney, simply saw him as extra 'muscle' placed there, in case any punters took umbrage to losing, and not aware that Francis had been placed by Garvin to keep an eye on matters. Francis watched Mooney just 'like a hawk' for the remainder of that day, as the weather dried and the game of 'pitch and toss' continued. Offers of treble bets and other such enticements were being generously offered by Mooney, in an attempt to persuade punters to win back any losses. As Francis further observed the odds being altered by Mooney, at several intervals during the day. Any punters daring to challenge Mooney about this, were all met with the usual threat of violence, and an ejection from 'Sky Edge.'

At around four o'clock that afternoon, gambling had ceased for the day, and the Park men then made their way down toward the Durham Ox public house, located on Broad Street. Mooney seemed to be in a celebratory mood, as he paid for a leg of lamb to be cooked by the landlady, for the Park men. All continued to enjoy several pints courtesy of the pub landlord, in order to keep in their favour, and all were soon in a boisterous mood, as they waited for the pork to be served. As the beer flowed, a disagreement then developed between Frank Kidnew and Amos Ridley over a previous unpaid money debt. Other drinkers within the Durham Ox already sensing trouble, had now began to leave the pub, and soon both men were squaring up toward each other. Francis then decided to intervene as he got between both men, and much to the annoyance of Mooney, who saw this as a liberty being taken by the outsider.

The attention now turned toward Francis, who was now challenged by Mooney to a fight outside the pub. He had not expected events to turn this sour and so quickly, it was quite obvious that Mooney had a grudge with the unfamiliar Francis. George Wheyhill stepped in and tried to calm Mooney down, but he had become so wound up that he attempted to punch Francis whilst still inside the pub. No matter how much Wheyhill tried to avert matters Mooney would not listen, as Francis realised that he could not back down from this confrontation.

He proceeded to go through the pub door directly to the street outside, followed by Mooney. He walked directly behind Francis when he suddenly crouched downward, and picked up a wooden table stool. As he then proceeded to hit the unaware Francis, with the stool across the back of his head. Francis was knocked across the pavement, and into the path of an Omnibus that was heading up Broad Street. Quite dazed at the unexpected blow, he observed the Omnibus heading in his direction, as he jumped up to his feet, and went straight at Mooney with a punch directly toward his head. This time it was Mooney that was caught unprepared, as the blow saw the back of Mooney's head, hit the stone window sill of the pub. Both men were now suffering cuts to the head area, as blood was clearly visible from both head wounds. Mooney responded as he came back toward Francis like a man who was 'possessed,' with rage, and dealing several blows from both fists. As all Francis could now do was to back up against the pub wall, and hold a defensive stance in shielding his head from the relentless, fast blows of Mooney.

A crowed had now gathered around both men to watch the fight, as Francis was able to withstand Mooney's blows, he could sense that Mooney was tiring, when he suddenly raised up and began his own offensive, in his response back toward Mooney. The strength of Francis could see Mooney being backed off with successive blows to his head and face, both men were now brawling in the middle of Broad Street, with carts and several other traffic all being brought to a standstill. Francis could now be seen to be getting the better of Mooney, but was also cautious that Mooney might produce a weapon if he let up in his assault toward him. He was about to administer another blow, toward

Mooney when he was grabbed around the neck by both Frank Kidnew, and Sam Garvin, as he was wrestled down onto the cobbles. Kidnew had been to fetch Garvin from nearby Bard Street as the fight began, and this was much to the relief of Mooney, who had taken quite a beating from him. As Francis lay on the cobbles, trying to gather his breath, when he could see Mooney now coming back toward him, with a poker held up in the air. Garvin then hit Mooney directly into the stomach, as he then keeled over, and dropped the poker as a result of the blow.

This situation was not good for both fugitives, as a large crowd had gathered, and Garvin did not want to alert any attention of the Police to the incident. Garvin quickly began shouting orders toward the Park men, and them all to get Mooney back inside the Durham Ox, to which they had soon reacted. Garvin and Wheyhill both helped the injured Francis back to Mary Parkin's house on Bard Street, where Mary then tended to Francis's wounds.

"That paddy is getting out of fucking order, and tekin liberties like this" said Garvin.

"You had him William, he weren't coming back from that" added Wheyhill.

Wheyhill then left the house to check out the situation back at the Durham Ox, with Garvin to follow him ten minutes later if was all clear, and no Police around.

"Thats nothing to what I noticed earlier, when you go back to divvy up tell me how much, as I saw him altering odds" replied Francis.

"Just as I thought he might be doing, the Irish bastard, Ill sort him" replied Garvin.

After ten minutes Garvin had left the house, as he headed back up toward the Durham Ox, to meet with the others. Wheyhill had already gone ahead, and not returned back to Bard Street so the situation all seemed to have calmed with no Police in attendance.

Francis remained at Mary Parkin's house, where gently she tended to his wounds. She was so gentle toward him, as he began to feel quite relaxed in her company. She was an attractive woman in her late twenties, and he could see as to how Garvin was attracted toward her. It was so different for Francis to be in the company of such a woman, and a contrast to the brutal world that he had earlier frequented, in both France and Sheffield. She made him feel so much at ease, even though his head wound was quite painful to be touched. But Mary could be so gentle and delicate in everything that she did, she was quite talkative, and this also made Francis feel more at ease within her company. Just like himself, she had also originated from Lincolnshire, a small village near to Sleaford called East Heckington, her maiden name being Struggles. He had heard of several farmers known by that name, whilst working at Boston market. She told him that she had married young, and with her late husband had moved to Sheffield to find work in 1912. Her husband had also been an agricultural labourer just like Francis, but with the advent of mechanisation and the downturn in work, had forced them to move to Sheffield to find work. He had been killed just before the war, in a steelworks accident, as Mary was forced to take several part time jobs, in an attempt to support both herself and her two small children, as no compensation money would be paid by the company, for the loss of her husband.

Francis was so at ease with Mary, and they had so much in common, although the had never met before they appeared to be like long lost friends when they talked. He certainly felt attracted toward her, and he began to ponder, as to what she saw in the brutish and often selfish Sam Garvin. She was interested to hear about his family back in Sibsey Northlands, and of the stories surrounding his own life, living in the Fens.

Garvin had returned to the Durham Ox, to find a heavily bandaged George Mooney sat eating pork, along with the other Park men, as the pub descended into silence as Garvin entered.

"You are out of fucking order" angrily shouted Garvin, as he pointed toward Mooney.

"Little boy blue, not with yer then" he replied.

"You were lucky Frank fetched me, otherwise you were heading for the fucking Infirmary" said Garvin.

"Fuck off, my poker would have finished, that Lincoln bastard" replied Mooney.

This was so typical of Mooney, in assuming that he had beaten Francis, and was willing to boast to anyone willing to listen, even though all of the Park men knew he was heading for a beating, until Garvin and Wheyhill had intervened.

"Pull a fuckin stroke like that again, and Ill finish this me sen, I told yer to keep it quiet, whilst the coppers are about, and you pick a fight in the middle of Broad Street" said Garvin shaking his head.

"Fuck him back off to Lincoln, or wherever he comes from" replied Mooney.

At this remark, Garvin then stood over Mooney who remained seated, as he grabbed him by his bandaged head, and forcing his face down onto the wooden table.

"Ill fuck him back off to Lincoln, when I want to, I choose who's on this payroll, do yer fucking understand" as Garvin now used more force onto Mooney's bandaged head, against the table.

"Yes," came the muffled response from Mooney, as Garvin quickly let go, and had soon asserted his authority with Mooney.

Garvin asked for the days takings, as he paid out the shares to each of the Park men. Mooney was always paid more for overseeing matters at Sky Edge, but as Garvin was now back he explained this would no longer now be necessary. Mooney felt so humiliated, and was soon on the offensive of accusing Frank Kidnew of grinning at Garvin's humiliation of him.

"Also wi what thas been tekin, should meek up thi wages" said Garvin.

Mooney subdued and scorned, then simply turned toward the others and shouted "yer fucking Park bastards" as he left the pub.

He made his way down Broad Street, toward the city centre, where he attacked an innocent man who was simply walking in the opposite direction, and for no reason but to vent his anger. After the assault he ran off in the direction of Exchange Street, his head still bandaged, and the wound bleeding.

Garvin stayed on for a drink with the remainder of the Park men, as several surprisingly admitted to him, that they were aware of the odds lowering scam. Garvin was livid at hearing this and that only George Wheyhill had the bottle to report this to him. The Park men remained silent, as Garvin just stared at them.

He turned to Frank Kidnew,"Frankie why?" he asked.

"He threatened to cut me Sam" replied Kidnew.

"Yer all supposed to be fucking Park men" shouted Garvin.

"You were supposed to be looking after the ring, whilst I was in the fuckin Army, and that fucking Paddy was taking liberties all along. I also trusted the Irish bastard, like av been an idiot. But apart from George, none of yer had the fuckin bottle to pull him up" as he angrily addressed the group.

"I want yer all up at the Edge at nine tomorrow, ill risk running things from now, with George and William to be trusted with the money. Anybody, and I mean anybody crosses me, and ill come for yer" at this Garvin drank the remainder of his beer, and walked out of the pub, and onto Broad Street.

He was soon back at the house on Bard Street, where he approached the rear door to Mary's house, as he could hear laughter coming from the inside. As he opened the door, both Mary and Francis were sat at the table, with Francis playing with one of the children. As Garvin entered the room the mood quickly changed, he was so angry at the earlier events in the Durham Ox, as he began to tell Francis the story. Mary then picked up the child, and made an excuse to nip out for some bread, at the nearby grocers shop. Garvin didn't seem concerned as to how Mary and Francis had been getting along so well, but was more concerned with the antics of George Mooney, and how he had took advantage of him whilst being away. They talked for a while as to how Garvin wanted 'Sky Edge' to be better organised, as he barely noticed, as Mary returned home from the shop.

Francis thought it was time for him to return back to the lodging house, but Mary insisted he stay on for something to eat, to which Garvin half heartedly agreed, his mind obviously still on matters that had happened earlier. Francis stayed for the food prepared by Mary, and he was more than happy to spend more time there, as they both chatted about life back in Lincolnshire. Garvin typically ignored them both, and went into the sitting room, with a newspaper,whilst she prepared the food.

Mooney now blamed Francis for all of this scenario and of his ousting, and wanted to extract his revenge, he knew that to declare him to the authorities as a deserter, would certainly have to involve the naming of Garvin, and he dare not risk this. He knew that he was still living at the lodging house off Scotland Street, now that Garvin was living on Bard Street, he would have to return home alone at some point later that evening.

Mooney had arrived back at Trinity Street, his wife shocked at his appearance, and of him being swathed in a bandage around his weeping head wound. She slowly removed the bandage, the wound had clearly opened up, and was still bleeding. She could only advise him to visit the Infirmary for some further treatment, and to have the wound sewn. Mooney was so reluctant to do this, and only wanted to further settle the score with Francis. Unlike Garvin he was not as such an intelligent man, and any confrontation like this, soon became his only focus and to extract his revenge. His wife pleaded with him to have the wound treated immediately, as he would occasionally lose his balance, whenever he tried to stand. But in Mooney's stubbornness, he ignored his wife and soon was making his way up toward the St Vincent's Catholic Working Mens Club, at Croft House. His reputation and the respect afforded to him within the Irish community, meant that Mooney would easily be able to recruit other like minded individuals, to assist with the settling of the score with Francis. There was already some bad feeling from the Irish community toward Francis, following the earlier incident at the Queens Hotel.

Mooney knew of two brothers who regularly drank in the club called John and Patrick Quinn, who both had quite a fearsome reputation as fighters within the West Bar area, and could be easily influenced to participate in something like this, for the price of a pint. It wasn't long before the Quinn's were sat drinking with Mooney, as he requested their services. The Quinn's were also friends with the young guy who had been attacked and cut by Garvin, but they were soon convinced by Mooney, that it was Francis who was the main instigator in that incident.

It was soon time for Francis to return back to the lodging house, as he bid goodnight to Mary and Garvin, and he walked off down Broad Street, toward Exchange Street. It was now dark outside, as he was feeling quite upbeat, as he couldn't help but think of Mary, and as to how they had got along so well, from that first meeting. He continued along Campo Lane, as he then took a shortcut across Paradise Square, and on toward Scotland Street. All seemed unusually quiet on Scotland Street, as he walked past the Queens Hotel. He was still in some pain from the earlier confrontation with Mooney, and was now looking forward to a good nights sleep in order to recover.

He turned into the courtyard of the lodging house, where he soon noticed the outline of two figures stood within the shadow of the privies.

"Are you'se William Francis?" came a voice from out of the shadows

"And who wants to know?" he replied

"Me!" as he was then suddenly hit from behind, with what appeared to be a large coal shovel.

Falling down to the ground, the two assailants then began to hit Francis relentlessly with the shovel, he was unable to fight back given the ferocity of the attack, and was soon drifting out of consciousness, as he lay unable to move. A lone man then entered into the courtyard, as one of the attackers turned to him

"You'se seen fuck all, or you'se gets the same, now you go inside and don't come out"

The man quickly moved toward the door of one of the houses. The beating upon Francis continued even as he lay in his subconscious state, as both assailants then ran off toward the direction of Townhead Street. Francis laid there motionless, as soon three men came out from a house in the courtyard, and bent over Francis, to check he was still breathing. He was alive, and under the light of a candle the men could see that his head was badly swollen, and had been cut in several places on his torso, due to the ferocity of the attack with the coal shovel. One of the men ran out into Scotland Street, and headed toward the Police station on Water Lane, to report the assault and to summon an ambulance.

As the Police and ambulance arrived, it was highlighted that Francis's condition was serious, and he needed urgent Hospital treatment, to help reduce the swelling around his head. The ambulance headed off in the direction of the Infirmary, whilst the two Police Officers in attendance tried to take statements, none of the three men were willing to offer any statements, including the man who had earlier witnessed the assault. Even when they were advised that Francis might die, and this could result in a murder charge, no one was willing to give a statement, and just reiterated, that they had found him lying there in the courtyard.

At the Infirmary Francis was prepared for emergency surgery, as his bloodied clothes were cut away from his bruised and broken body. He was examined by the doctor, whose main concern was to reduce the swollen state, of his head, and of the possibility of brain pressure. Francis was in the operating theatre for nearly four hours as the medical staff, tried to stabilise his condition. Still in a state of unconsciousness he was taken to a mens ward, with the hope of him pulling through. His features were barely recognisable as a result of the assault, and several Hospital screens were placed around his bed, much to the inquisitive nature of the other patients residing within the ward. It was now only a matter of time and hope, that he would recover from this ordeal, and a return to his former self. He was monitored by the nursing staff on an hourly basis, and all they could do was try to make him as comfortable as was possible, as they all spoke to him as if he was conscious, in the hope this might trigger something within his subconscious.

The following day Garvin attended Sky Edge, and now so keen to stamp his mark on matters, following the issues that had arisen the previous day. He noticed there was no sign of Francis at the rings, and was quite curious as to why he hadn't shown up by ten o clock. The gambling continued for the remainder of the day, and this time supervised by Garvin and Wheyhill. After midday the elderly Irish man who ran the lodging house, came to see Garvin.

"Its William, he was jumped last night in the courtyard, the guy next door saw he was being attacked by two guys with a shovel. He was out cold, an ambulance was called and he is now in the Infirmary" as he spoke to Garvin.

"Who saw it?" he asked.

"One of the guys who lodges next door, come and see him after ten, as he is on afternoons" he replied.

"Is William still in the Infirmary?" asked Garvin.

"His bed wasn't slept in last night, so I assume so" he replied.

Garvin thanked the elderly Irish guy, as he gave him a half a crown for his trouble. Garvin then asked George Wheyhill and Amos Ridley to mind the rings for the remainder of that afternoon. As Garvin and Frank Kidnew, both set off toward the Infirmary, as boarded a tramcar on Duke Street and headed into the city centre. Within twenty minutes both men were walking through the front gardens of the City Infirmary, and into the large sandstone building. They walked into the large tiled entrance lobby, where they were greeted by a nurse who then advised them that no visitors were allowed, until after the evening meal. Garvin was angry at this news as he demanded to see the patient, who had been brought in the previous night.

She asked for his name, Frank Kidnew quickly responded with"William Fra_____," until he was quickly nudged and interrupted by Garvin.

"Its George, George Wheyhill" hastily replied Garvin

"Three, four court, South Street, Park"

"Is he all right, can we see him?" asked Garvin.

"That who he is" as she wrote down his name "Im afraid he's very poorly, and in recovery from the theatre, he was very badly injured from an assault, and has some severe swelling to his brain" replied the nurse.

"If you come back at six o clock, we might know some more" she added.

Garvin and Kidnew left back through the main doors, as they walked down toward Langsett Road, and waited at the tramcar stop.

"Who do you reckon?" asked Kidnew

"I have a feeling it's the fuckin Paddy's, and Mooney is getting one back at me, he didn't like being beat by William" replied Garvin.

"Ill go to the lodging house tonight after ten, to see the bloke who witnessed it" added Garvin.

The tramcar slowed to a halt, as both men jumped onto the rear platform, and sat down on the lower deck, to undertake the short journey along Shalesmoor and back toward Snig Hill. Both men then called for a drink in the Bell Hotel, before walking back along Broad Street, and into to the Park district. He returned to Bard Street, and told Mary of what had happened to Francis. She tried to ask Garvin further questions, but at this time he knew nothing more to tell her.

He decided to call in at George Wheyhill's house, and ask Wheyhill to visit Mooney, to see if he would let anything slip. Wheyhill told Garvin, he had already been to see him, and he let nothing slip out, as he told Wheyhill he knew nothing about it, and was home all night after his return from the Durham Ox.

Garvin asked if Wheyhill would accompany him later up to West Bar, to see the Irish fella who had witnessed the assault at ten o clock. Wheyhill agreed to go with Garvin, and the pair would meet up later, as Garvin returned home to Bard Street. Mary asked if she could go and visit Francis, to which he replied "no point he's out of it anyway, the Irish bastards, have done this, it has Mooney written all over it."

"What are you planning on doing?" she asked him.

"It was witnessed by an Irish guy, living next door to William, he's on afternoons so were gonna see him at ten, if he'll tell us owt" he replied.

He met Wheyhill in the Durham Ox, and after a couple of drinks, both set off in the direction of Scotland Street. It was now ten thirty as they entered into the courtyard and the scene of the assault, twenty-four hours earlier. They approached Francis's lodging house, and asked the elderly Irish owner if he could point out the guy who lodged next door. He went next door and walked inside, after a couple of minutes he returned in the company of another man, who he introduced to them as John Mulligan.

"Did tha see owt last night, and that bloke who got beat up?" asked Garvin.

"No, I didn't see anything, you must be mistaken, it wasn't me" he replied.

"He said it were" said Garvin, pointing over to the lodging house owner.

"Look I couldn't see anything in the dark, so just leave me be" he replied.

Wheyhill moved closer with the purpose of hitting the guy, until he would co-operate. Garvin raised his hand up to Wheyhill,

"Here's five pounds for you to tell us, we know it will be hard for you living here, theres no way no one else will know, apart from us four stood here" said Garvin

"Can we all goes into your house?" said Mulligan, as he asked the elderly lodging house owner

All four went into the lodging house, and then up to Francis's room. Once in the room, the Irish guy sat on the bed, and relayed what he knew to Garvin and Wheyhill.

"There were two of em, it was the brothers who drink in the Catholic Club up at the Crofts, I don't know their names, but their group always take over the billiards table in there" he told them.

Garvin passed him the five pounds in notes, and then assured him he wouldn't be mentioned, in any further undertaking. All three men came downstairs, then left the lodging house, as Mulligan returned next door.

Garvin and Wheyhill began the walk home, and the streets were now empty, as they discussed their plan of action, with a view to extract their revenge. Garvin couldn't be seen carrying out this attack, or he would be apprehended, he was going to have to use the other Park men. Wheyhill naturally was the first to volunteer to be part of the group, he had grown up with Garvin, and realised as to what he and Francis had experienced in France. He could be trusted by Garvin, to organise the others, to undertake this.

The following day Wheyhill attended the gambling ring as per usual, and he took both Frank Kidnew, and another Park man called Harold Keyworth to one side, for a quiet word. He explained the predicament of Francis, and of Garvin's wishes,to settle this score on his behalf, all three Park men were to be given five pounds each to undertake this, and would no doubt to be in the favour of Garvin. All that they knew of their intended victims, were that they were two Irish brothers, that played billiards, in the St Vincent's Catholic Club. They were all to meet later that night at seven o clock, in the Bell Hotel in Fitzalan

Square, and then to make their way up toward West Bar, and the Crofts.

All three men were carrying pokers, concealed within the lining of their jackets, as they walked calmly in the direction of West Bar. As they all walked along Scotland Street, they could sense the feeling of hostility toward them, as most outsiders would often feel in this part of town. They had soon reached the imposing stone archway, which led through to the cobbled courtyard of St Vincent's Church, as the doorway in the left hand corner of the courtyard, lead into the club. It was now eight thirty and the club was quite busy inside, with groups of men sat playing dominoes and cribbage, at several tables. It might have only been their imagination, but the club lounge just seemed to go quiet, as all three men walked in, and headed toward the bar. Wheyhill quickly surveyed the scene, and realised this was going to be difficult in launching an attack inside here, they had to get the brothers outside. He could see an archway, beyond which was a billiards room, and being separate to the main lounge. Keyworth ordered three pints at the bar, at which point the barman sensing trouble, refused to serve them on account of them not being members, or from the Irish community. From behind them one of the groups who were sat playing cards, came a voice in an Irish accent "give em all a drink," it was George Mooney, sat playing cards with the group, with his head still bandaged. He stood up and walked over to join all three at the bar.

"Here to do his dirty work, for him?" he asked.

"Fuck off George, you know why we are here" replied Wheyhill

Looking toward the billiard table, he asked Mooney "Well is it them two?"

There were two dark haired men, and with their dark skin tone looked quite similar to each other, as they were stood at the billiards table, with a group of three other men. All five were quite oblivious, and had not noticed, the three strangers who had now walked into the club.

"Depends what they have supposed to have done" replied Mooney.

"You fucking well know George, you were well out of order" said Wheyhill

"I'll tell you who's out of order! That fucking Garvin, and his Lincoln Army pal, it was all right up there, until they fuckin came back" replied Mooney in a raised tone.

Mooney's raised voice had alerted others to the heated conversation, and very soon Patrick Quinn came walking over.

"You'se all right George, who are these three fuckers" he asked him.

"No one, they were just going, now fuck off back to the Park all of you" replied Mooney.

Harold Keyworth now sensing that a situation was going to develop, clutched the poker on the inside of his jacket. Wheyhill also realising this, looked toward Keyworth and simply nodded, as Patrick Quinn then turned around to speak with his associates. Keyworth then struck Patrick Quinn on the back of the head with his poker, as Wheyhill and Kidnew then charged toward the other four men stood at the billiard table. Their pokers, and ferocity of the charge, meant that all four were very quickly disabled and were reeling about on the floor, in agony before they had any chance to react. Wheyhill and Kidnew were raining successive blows upon each man as they lay. Upon seeing

Patrick Quinn fall to the floor, Mooney then came at Keyworth who then hit him directly across his bandaged head, as he reeled backwards and over a table. Keyworth then joined the other two in the beating of the four men that included John Quinn, until Wheyhill held up his arm as all three stood back. He pulled out a razor, held it in the air, and in his breathless state said "our argument is with these two, so no one come fuckin near."

Keyworth then pulled Patrick Quinn up from the floor by his hair, as Kidnew held onto John Quinn by his collar, dragging both men to the outside courtyard of the club. John Quinn was soon screaming for mercy, and asking the other patrons for their help, as Wheyhill hit him again with his poker. No one moved inside the lounge, as Mooney had also been knocked unconscious, and was laid between a chair, and the table he was knocked over. The Quinn brothers were then thrown down on to the hard cobbles of the church courtyard, as both Keyworth and Kidnew continued with the merciless assault upon both brothers, using both boots, and pokers. Both were pleading with the Park men for mercy, as they continued with the beating. Soon Wheyhill had held up his arm for them to stop, he reached downward, firstly lifting John Quinn by the hair, and striking him across his cheek with his razor. John Quinn screamed out, as soon blood could be seen dripping onto the cobbles from his wound. Next was Patrick Quinn and a similar strike, with the razor directly across his face.

All three men quickly left the courtyard leaving both Quinn brothers laid out semi conscious upon the cobbled courtyard. They then hastily walked up Solly Street, and made their way toward Glossop Road and to the relative safety, away from the Crofts. All three men were now heavily perspiring and sweating in the cold night air following the physical assertion of the assault. So they made their way toward The Raven public house located at the top of Fitzwilliam Street, to compose themselves, and a much needed drink. Justice had been dealt by Garvin, as all three satisfied their task had been undertaken successfully.

The following morning Wheyhill called to see Garvin at Bard Street, to tell him of the previous nights events. Garvin looked so pleased and smirked, especially with the news of Mooney being knocked unconscious, in the struggle. Mary was listening to the conversation between Wheyhill and Garvin, as she asked Garvin if he wanted her to visit Francis at the Infirmary. He agreed with her that this would be useful, and to keep him informed, until Francis had regained some consciousness.

Mary was so pleased that he had agreed for her to do this, and it made her feel that she would be doing something useful, and be hopefully be contributing to the recovery of Francis. She left for the Infirmary at around five o clock, that evening for the visiting time. Upon arrival she asked the duty sister for the location of a Mr George Wheyhill within the Infirmary, and with the story that was earlier concocted by Garvin. She was directed by the sister, to the male ward located up on the second floor of the Infirmary as she explained to her that he was being nursed behind screens, given the seriousness of his condition.

She entered into the ward, and saw the screens that were surrounding the single bed. She rolled back the screen, and the shock of the view which met her, as she saw Francis laid on that bed, caused tears to well up in her eyes. Here was a young man of only twenty-one years of age, who had come through the ravages of the war in France being mostly unscathed, and was now on the verge of possibly dying at the hands of these thugs. His head bandaged, and the bruising to both his face and arms, so highlighted the ferocity of the beating he had taken. She sat by his bed side, as held onto his hand with tears now flowing down the side of her cheeks. Mary was at a loss about what to do in the short time that she had to spend here with William, in this unconscious state. Although she was not that much older than William she knew she needed to be there in a maternal role, as no doubt as his own mother would have been, if ever she knew of this ordeal. William Francis was a strong man, as she kept repeating to herself, over and over again. She also knew that in herself she had possibly developed some feelings toward William, in the all too brief time she had come to know him.

As she held onto his hand, all she could do was to talk of her earlier life in the Fens, from her own upbringing in East Heckington, life on her father's farm, skating on the frozen dykes, the harvest, school time, and of Boston market, anything she could possibly think of, no matter how trivial, as she knew how this earlier life meant so much to William. She was openly crying as she kept wiping her tears away as she talked away, and hoping that none of the nurses would see her in this state. She continued with her talking, as William just lay there with no movement.

Soon visiting time came to an end, as she composed herself and prepared to leave the Hospital ward, she bent over William kissed him on his cheek, and made her way back through the screens, and out onto the ward.

A hand bell had earlier been rung, to highlight that visiting time was now over, as several other visitors made their way out of the ward, and onto the stairwell leading down toward the entrance. Mary hurried, as she could now see a tramcar approaching, from further along Langsett Road through the stairwell window. She would visit him again tomorrow, and to pray for him, in the hope that he would be able to pull through all of this, and with no permanent damage.

As she returned back to Bard Street, Garvin had left the children alone, and gone to the Durham Ox no doubt to discuss the day's activities with the others. She couldn't expect him to do much more, as they weren't his own children, so she gave both children supper, and spent some time reading with them, as she put them both to bed. It wasn't long before she began to snooze in front of the range, as she was abruptly woken by Garvin, returning home from the Durham Ox at around ten o clock, and was asking for his supper. She duly obliged, by making him some bread and pork dripping sandwiches, and retired herself to bed. She was soon followed by Garvin, as he climbed into the bed at her side and he was soon snoring away, as she could think of nothing else but William, and as to how she so wished it was him, that was there lying there.

The following morning as she got up, she made up and lit the range, as she prepared breakfast for Garvin and the children. Yet again her thoughts were elsewhere, as all she could think about was William laid in that Hospital bed, and her anger at the whole scenario.

Garvin had given the Hospital, the name of George Wheyhill as the injured patient, as he assumed that the Hospital would relay any information about William Francis back to the Police. Who would highlight Francis's whereabouts to the Military Police. As she had promised Francis on that previous day, Mary again attended the visiting hour at the Infirmary, but this time as she entered the ward the screens were missing, and no one was laid on the bed. Her heart sank, as she became weak and unstable desperately holding onto the bed, as her eyes began to well up. She couldn't help but to stare at the empty bed, as she slowly walked toward the matrons room located at the far side of the ward.

She knocked at the door and entered into the room, the matron was an elderly buxom lady, possibly in her late fifties, as she turned to look up at Mary from her desk.

"William, Willian Francis" unable to hide her tears as she spoke quietly, to the matron

"Sorry, no William Francis on my ward" she replied back to her.

Mary had to re-compose herself, and then remembered the conversation between Wheyhill, and Garvin around his identity, as she wiped the tears away from her eyes.

"Sorry George Wheyhill is he dead" she asked her, physically shaking as she awaited her response.

"No dear, he has gone back down to the theatre earlier this afternoon, and he has woken up. Were you the lady who visited him yesterday?" she asked.

"Yes" as the tone of her voice now lifted and so upbeat, at the relief of this news.

"After you had left, he just sat up and began talking to one of the nurses. From the early signs he seems to be ok, and able to function, count, and see properly, there is still some severe swelling to the head, and they have taken him back down to theatre, to try to relieve this" she replied.

"Will he be back up soon" asked Mary.

"I wouldn't think so, not before visiting time finishes, I would come back tomorrow" replied the matron.

At this news Mary ran out of the ward and back down the steps, it was raining outside but in her elation at this news she couldn't be contained, as she ran over to the tramcar stop across from the Infirmary gates. She took the tramcar back toward the city centre, as she walked the short journey home to Bard Street, as the rain poured, and quite oblivious to this, so happy at the thought of Williams recovery. She reached Bard Street, but decided to let Garvin know of this news, so she made her way straight to the Durham Ox public house, where she knew Garvin would be. Outside the Durham Ox she saw Frank Kidnew who was about to enter the pub, she asked if he would tell Sam to come outside. Garvin came outside as she relayed the news from the Infirmary, as tears now appeared in her eyes, such was her elation that he was making such a recovery. Garvin responded to her, by simply saying "good," as he then turned away, and walked back inside the pub.

Mary returned to her house on Bard Street, again unable to contain her joy, as she hugged both children. She decided to retire early to bed herself as the 'rollercoaster' of emotions from the day, had tired her considerably. Garvin returned much later, as he woke her to demand his supper, as she duly obliged, and again her thoughts being on the next day, to hopefully talk with William.

She visited him again on the following day, and was so pleased to be back in his company, and him being conscious. During their conversation, their hands briefly brushed against each other, as William then moved his hand backward, as he held on to Mary's hand. This highlighted an exchange of affection from him toward her, that was soon replicated by Mary. They were so at ease with each others company, and just like before, chatted as if they had known each other for several year's. Before long it was time for visiting to finish, as the hand bell was sounded. They continued to hold hands, as Mary leant over Francis, and kissed him gently on the cheek. She was told by the matron that they would consider his discharge in two more days. Mary continued to visit him for the duration of his time that he was in the Infirmary, and after three further days the doctor was satisfied with his progress, that he could be discharged.

To Mary's concern, he was to return back to the lodging house, following his discharge from the Infirmary. Garvin, Wheyhill, and Keyworth, had all visited Mooney earlier on the day of his discharge, and following reassurances from Mooney, Francis was to be left alone whilst he was living back in West Bar. Garvin then also agreed for Mooney to return back up to 'Sky Edge' as both men then shook hands over the agreement. Francis returned to the lodging house with both Garvin and Wheyhill, as Garvin had arranged for a food hamper and some new clothes to be delivered up to his room. Francis then spent the following two days resting, only leaving the house to visit the privy, and quickly returning back up to his room. Within a week of this convalescence period, he now felt ready to return to make his way back to 'Sky Edge.' Garvin had visited to see how he was recovering, and had arranged for Wheyhill to collect him on the following morning, with a view to escorting him up to 'Sky Edge.'

Given both his strength and physical prowess Francis had made such a fast recovery, and was quickly back to his old self as he highlighted little pain as the bruising and other injuries subsided. He showed no animosity toward George Mooney during this period, although their relationship still remained quite 'frosty,' as they simply acknowledged each other with their dealings at 'Sky Edge.'

Matters soon had settled down and returned back to a degree of normality, and on the following week both Francis and Garvin attended Sky Edge, on the fateful morning of the Military Police raid. Both were apprehended by the Military Police for their 'desertion of duty,' whilst serving with the West Riding regiment in France, and were both returned under escort back to the Catterick Garrison to await their punishment.

Chapter 7 - Return to France.

The arrest of Garvin and Francis, following the raid of 'Sky Edge' undertaken by both the Sheffield City Police, and the Military Police, led to both men being detained at Catterick Garrison in the North Riding of Yorkshire. Ten days later, they were both transferred to the notorious Army prison camp at Devizes in Wiltshire, known to all as the 'Glasshouse'. After three weeks of intense 'Army drill' at Devizes, and as a direct result of their previous service records, both men were given the option of either returning back to France and the completion of their Army service, with one year of 'hard labour' commuted, until after the war had ended. Or if this option was to be refused, to face a full Army trial, where the possible outcome could possibly be death by firing squad, for desertion.

Both men agreed on an immediate return back to France, and to an attachment to the 51st Highlanders, whom they were to join, near to Paris. From Devizes, they were both escorted by the Military Police back to London, and to the onward train toward Dover, where they were then placed under the custody of the royal navy. Word had soon got around the boat as to why both men were being apprehended, and soon cat calls and other such derogatory remarks, were being aimed toward both men, by other Soldiers travelling on the boat. Garvin was able to simply shun this, or to respond with some other quip in return. But Francis being the more studious of the pair, took a lot of this hostility to heart. It was possibly only the presence of the two royal marines in attendance that were to guard over them, that had possibly saved either man from an assault or even worse, such was the bad feeling generated toward deserters.

The boat docked in Calais, and the men were subsequently handed back over to the Military Police and escorted to a waiting train to begin their journey back toward the front line. This time the rail journey was a much quieter affair, as the train made its way toward Reims located in Marne. The train never halted during the journey between Calais and Reims, and after around three hours of travelling the familiar flashes and the lighting of the night sky, was being witnessed from the carriage windows.

Upon their arrival at Reims, the Soldiers were immediately ordered off the train, and ordered to line up on the station platform, they both soon realised that they were now very near to the front line, with the sound of exploding shells and gunfire, echoing in the night sky. The sound had made Garvin become uneasy, as he began to swear and curse quietly to himself, Francis was apprehensive as to what experience awaited them with the Highlanders, and their arrival back at the front line. The majority of the Soldiers that had travelled on the train with them, were new arrived recruits from the same West Riding regiment. As all the men were lined up on the station platform, both Francis and Garvin naturally began to feel that they were now to be drafted back into Garvin's old regiment. But the Army, as always kept to its word, and soon after the roll call, both men were then asked to step forward, and to follow an Officer into another building, located toward the end of the rail platform. Here they were briefed by the Officer, who told them that they were both to be taken over to a Commanding Officer of the 51st Highland regiment, and to report to him for duty.

Both men climbed aboard the back of an open Army truck, stood idling outside of the station building, with Garvin and Francis being the only passengers on board, as it slowly began its journey over the unmade and pot holed road, in the stark darkness of the French countryside. Both men sat on the back of the truck observing the flashes, screeching and explosions, echoing in the darkness high above them. Flares continually lit up the night sky, highlighting a haunting green tinge of light, and this was quickly followed by the reverberating sound of machine gun fire, as the flare now fell back down toward the ground. Here, they soon realised that this was not a quiet sector of the front line, and they had no doubt that they were to soon re-enter the trenches. The truck then abruptly came to a halt in the middle of an area of woodland, as both men were ordered to disembark, and then to proceed further following the road on foot, and to ensure that no visible light was highlighted from either of them. Francis had earlier remarked to Garvin as to how the driver of the truck, had managed to drive this far in the total darkness, and with no lighting to assist him, aside from the flares being fired in the distance. They were told to follow the unmade road for about another two miles, before they would reach a series of communication trenches, and to report to, the first Officer they came across.

The smell of sulphur and burning now became so much stronger as they neared toward the trench system, as they could hear voices shouting in the distance of the still night air. They were walking through an area of woodland, as yet unscathed by the effects of shellfire. Only the occasional sound of a shell and of other shrapnel landing nearby, made them realise they were now within the German range. Several stretcher bearers were being passed heading from the opposite direction and carrying injured men, away from the front, many in a great deal of distress. Francis could hear Garvin swearing and cursing to himself as they passed by, as he began to realise that this return to the front, was beginning to have a profound effect, upon Garvin's wellbeing.

They reached a small platoon of men, sat sheltering just off the roadway toward the edge of the woodland.

"Where's a Commanding Officer?" asked Francis.

"None here laddie, were waiting for one, from the trenches" a man from the group replied to him in a strong Scottish accent.

"You'se guys Sherwood's, I am hearing your accent" he asked Francis.

"No, I was with Lincs, but we lost so many, so they attached me to the Yorkies" replied Francis.

"Wese been waiting for an hour now, were out collecting the wounded, normally Fritz is obliging about this and we hold fire, but tonight he exploded one so we had to move into these woods, and have all managed to get back and re-group over here" he replied.

He could see there were around thirty men, and all were sat in relative silence, as he quickly observed that in the faint light that they were wearing kilts. These were the Highlanders, as Garvin then asked if any could see to passing him a swig of whisky from the flasks, that he knew that they all carried. One Soldier duly obliged, as Garvin appeared a little calmer after this.

"What you Yorkies doing down here? they are all to the north of us" he then asked Garvin

"We were sent here in error by top brass at t' station but now were here, might as well report" replied Garvin hastily.

None of the other men raised any suspicion at this comment, and now the sound of breaking branches could be heard in the woods, toward the rear of their position, as someone else could be heard approaching the group. The Highland men all stood, with a view to challenging who ever this was. Both Francis and Garvin hadn't been issued with rifles at this point, so were both apprehensive as to what they could do in these circumstances, and if this approach happened to be a German. All of the men's fears were quickly relaxed, when the shout of 'friend,'that came through the darkness. From his English and upper class accent, it was obvious that this man was an Officer.

"Right, how many have we, and wheres the sergeant?" he asked

"Not here sir, only corporal McIntyre, and he was so badly injured, and has been taken back to the field station" replied a Soldier.

"Theres two more men here from the West Riding's, who say they have been sent up to join us" pointing in the direction of both Francis and Garvin. The Officer approached both men in the darkness.

"Names?" he asked them.

"Francis and Garvin sir, reporting to join the 51st Highlanders as instructed" replied Francis.

"Right, fall in with the rest of the men. We are going to have to get back into the communication trench, before light, We are a sitting target for Fritz here" as he addressed the group.

"I suggest we crawl forward in pairs across the open ground, and complete silence when out there, and we just hope they don't send up a flare"

Toward the front of the woodland, and in the direction of the German line, was a small open field, it was obvious now that the men were to crawl across this field and keeping low, in order to reach the relative safety of the communication trench at the opposite side of the field. The field sloped slightly downward toward the communication trench, but it was in full view of a German machine gun post. Rather than charge the one hundred or so yards across the field and back toward the trench system, where they all ran the risk of all being mowed down, should the Germans notice any such movement. It was decided to slowly move across the open ground in pairs, in the hope that the German gun would not notice any such sudden movement. This was such a risky undertaking, and if any movement was spotted, it would be an inevitable death to the poor souls caught out in the middle of the open ground.

Two of the Highlanders had volunteered to go first, as they slowly dropped down to the ground, to begin the slow crawl out of the line of trees, and keeping their bodies as low as was possible in the darkness. Everybody watched with anticipation as they slowly moved forward, and hoping they would be unnoticed or of the unfortunate timing of a flare being launched.

Both men successfully made it as they dropped out of view and into the safety of the communication trench. The next two men now left the wood, yet this time approached moving four yards quickly, then halting for a several seconds, as this method appeared to be much faster on reaching the trench, than the steady crawl, and both men were soon dropping in the trench. Francis and Garvin watched the events unfold in anticipation, and quite concerned that a flare had not been fired for some time, and of the real possibility of this happening upon their own turn. Several pairs of men had successfully negotiated the open space, and it was soon their turn to head toward the trench system, as yet no flare had been fired. They had both decided to adopt the faster method of approach, and so set off in successive four yard spurts and halts. Francis soon noticed that Garvin had began to curse quietly toward himself once they out in the open ground, as he turned toward him and quietly told him to shush. Both continued their movement and soon the edge of the trench was visible, but Garvin continued to quietly swear and curse, as both moved forward. One of the Highlanders already in the trench, could hear Garvin's mutterings as he approached as both men then dropped over into the parapet of the service trench. In the darkness and confusion of the tumble, he grabbed hold of Garvin as he dragged him further along the trench, and well away from the movement of the men still coming across. Francis followed both of them, and realised something was wrong as Garvin would have normally reacted to the action of this Soldier dragging him along in this way, and was showing no resistance toward the Highland Soldier.

The Soldier pushed Garvin down into the mud of the trench, as he hit him at the side of his head with his fist, Francis just couldn't comprehend as to how Garvin hadn't reacted, as he held him by the throat "When you're told to keep quiet, you keep fucking quiet lad and not put the others in danger" as he threw him back toward the ground, Garvin just picked himself up and followed the others away from the edge of the trench, as they sat waiting for the Officer, and the other men to make their turn across the open land.

Garvin just didn't seem to be right, or his usual confident self, he would normally have reacted to this provocation and attacked the Highland Soldier, but he quietly sat down beside Francis. The men were sat waiting for the remaining Soldiers to cross, when unexpectedly a flare was fired, lighting up the ground and night sky. All of the men in the trench leaped down to the wet mud of the trench floor as they heard the reverberating sound of the German machine gun burst into life. Two poor souls had been caught out and were in full sight of the German guns, as they had crawled toward the trench, their bodies cut to pieces, as the bullets swept along the open land. Bullets were soon hitting the rear wall of the trench above them, as the men lay in the cold mud of the trench floor. Through the light of the flare, the German machine gunner had also spotted the remainder of the men preparing to cross the open land, as they crouched waiting their turn in the shelter of the wood. This proved to be no hiding place or sanctuary of shelter, as the bullets just ricocheted and mowed down the six remaining men. Screams could be heard coming from the direction of the woodland where only five minutes earlier, both Garvin and Francis had been stood, and awaiting their turn to cross the open ground.

Nothing could be done for any of the injured and dying men, as the group had to listen to their agonising screams, once the bullets had temporary subsided. They're only hope would be, if that they were able enough to crawl back toward the roadway, in the hope that other personal might be passing further along, and away from the front line. The service trenches were connected to the main deeper trench systems, in which safer shelter could be reached by the men. There were several other service trenches located further down the line to which supplies and arms, could be delivered toward the front line. The Germans strategically knew that by destroying, or covering the service trenches with gun sights, would have more of an effect upon the function and moral of the unit, rather than just simply attacking the trench.

As the firing subsided the remaining twenty or so men, proceeded along the service trench for around three yards, until the main trench fortifications were reached. The men fell into line and were immediately briefed by another Officer, who asked them about the earlier situation, and also of the acquisition of Garvin and Francis, within their platoon.   A member of the Highlanders relayed to the Officer the story and of the possible loss of the other men, and the Commanding Officer, who were last seen at the woodland. The platoon of Highlanders had been into 'no man's land' earlier that night collecting the injured, and it was noticed that even the Germans were doing likewise, with their injured. When suddenly a lone German machine gun post began picking off the stretcher bearers, as they worked. Their group was quickly scattered, with many of the Highlanders taking direct hits from the gun as they tried to flee. The only route of escape was through to the woodland, located to the right hand side of the trench system. Although the woodland was located on the British side of the front line, the men were always susceptible to German gun fire, given the slightly elevated position of the woodland.

The Officer approached Francis and Garvin, and it was fortunate he was not aware of the circumstances regarding their deployment to the Highlanders, yet was mystified as to them reporting for duty with the Highlanders, with the West Ridings being stationed, only two miles along the front line. Yet they were viewed as a welcome addition, to supplement the men they had already lost. Things quietened down later that morning, and as the sun rose its warmth adding to the otherwise miserable existence in the cold of that trench. Apart from the odd exploding shell nothing stirred from the German trench, so both men managed some much needed sleep, as they dozed against the relative dry area of a fire step.

At four o clock the call went up for 'ration time' as the men formed a queue to a tarpaulin covered section, in a rear trench. Underneath the tarpaulin was a cast iron portable stove, to which the men received a ladle of hot soup, and a crust of stale bread. Everything was devoured hastily by the men, and to ensure it was warm as they ate it. The smell of the soup had also attracted several rats, and caused them to drop into the trench system from the 'no man's land' up above. These were seen as sport by the men, as they were chased, often bayoneted, or hit by a rifle butt. Their carcasses then thrown upward, and over the top of the trench parapet, often being shot at by the Germans, much to the amusement and cheers from the Highlanders, in relieving their boredom

Neither Garvin nor Francis had yet been issued with a rifle, as they couldn't understand why, as it soon became clear, following on from the visit of another Officer to their sector, that they were to be allocated their specific duties for that night, and would not be needing a rifle. There had been a shell strike in another sector of the trench system, and several men had been badly injured and buried in the collapsed earth. Men had been frantically digging from each side of the debris for the past hour, but the majority of the other men were trapped further along, toward the centre of the shell strike.

Six men including both Francis and Garvin were to go out into 'no man's land' after nightfall in an attempt to extract the buried men, who lay near to the centre of the explosion. The prospect already filled them both with dread, at the thought of being such an open target for the German guns, and the feint hope that the Germans would respect that this, was an unarmed rescue party. Nightfall fell, as the six men only armed with field shovels, climbed the ladder over the parapet, and out of the trench system into the 'no man's land'. Garvin could again be heard muttering obscenities quietly to himself, as they hastily moved along the pockmarked and uneven ground. In the faint light they could see that bodies were laid in several places, along their route, following the front of the damaged trench wall. These men had been unable to be retrieved following the onslaught of the previous night's battle. Their smell was horrendous, and as the rescue party crawled between them, as a few faint groans could be heard from the bodies. Much to their relief the centre of the explosion had created a shell hole, which enabled the men to work, with some form of protection, and without the fear of being an open target for the German guns. They found one man still alive as they dug around him and Francis was able to pull him free from the mud, and earth.

Francis using all of his strength, then dragged the man by keeping himself low, and back along to the main trench system, as he then rolled him over the side to relative safety, and then quickly returned back to join Garvin, at the shell hole. They then located another man who was also still alive, and managed to free him, whilst Francis again dragged him back over to the trench. As Francis now reached the main trench, a flare was fired up into the night sky by the Germans, and suddenly machine guns reverberated back into life. Garvin was left stranded in the shell hole, whilst Francis quickly dived back down into the main trench, landing on top of the man, he had just rescued. As the light from the flare diminished on its return to the ground, screams could now be heard, coming from the direction of the shell hole to which Garvin was trapped. All Francis could do now, was to wait patiently until matters subsided again, and attempt to get back over to the shell hole. The calm returned after about thirty minutes, when the German firing ceased, as he cautiously lifted his head over the parapet of the trench and nothing stirred. He crawled back over toward the shell hole, with no further incident from the Germans, but what he found soon shocked him.

There were now three Soldiers in the shell hole, Garvin and two of the other Highlanders who were both dead, as he presumed had been shot in the light of the earlier flare. Garvin was laid onto his side in a foetal position, and holding his hands over his ears. He was shaking profusely and just kept repeating softly to himself "No more, no more, no more," over, and over again. Francis rolled him back over and onto his back, he told him he was here to save him, and was to take him back over to the trench, to which he grabbed tightly onto to Francis's arm. To the side of the shell hole was another dead body, that was now laying under several large rats feeding from the flesh of his face, and other open wounds , if there was ever an image of 'hell on earth' this is what Francis thought he was now enduring, and this had caused Garvin to breakdown. Here was a strong, fearless, and intelligent individual who had been reduced to a shadow of his former self, by him being sent back to the front line, and being something he could not cope with again.

As he had with the other injured men, Francis then dragged Garvin back to the main trench unscathed ,where both fell back in. Francis knew he had heard the cries of another man at the shell hole, and so he carefully went back up the ladder, and crawled back toward the shell hole. Another injured man could be seen peering through a small hole in the earth, he frantically dug, and again was able to pull out this man and drag him back to the safety of the main trench. All of the injured men including Garvin were then carried out of the front trench system, to a small dressing station located at the rear of the trench system, where each man was laid awaiting treatment. Garvin continued with his erratic behaviour, and continued repeating "no more, no more" to himself, he was shaking quite badly so Francis sat by his side, with his arm placed around him, until he was seen by the medical Officer. Garvin was quickly assessed by the medical Officer, and was deemed as unfit to continue in his role, and was to be escorted away from the front line for further treatment and recuperation. That was the last time he saw Garvin in France, and had no idea of his welfare, until he received a letter several weeks later from Mary Parkin, who explained that after some convalescence he had been allotted to logistical duties, and was later stationed near to Calais, and well away from the front line action.

Francis continued to serve with the Highlanders, and aside from his odd venture out into 'no mans land' usually on reconnaissance or wire repair work, this part of the front line saw little further action, as the Germans had retreated, and soon abandoned their trench system. Following a rest period behind lines, the Highlanders returned back to the front line. The Germans had abandoned everything, and had disappeared overnight, the Highlanders, were tasked to clear the battlefield of bodies, and of any land mines or other equipment being left behind by the Germans. He began to question if this was any worse than life being under fire, as he soon became hardened to the pitiful sight of the many mangled, and decomposed Soldiers left from the battle. The company were all due for a period of leave and relief from the front line, as the next few days became endless with boredom, and no sign of the enemy returning given the heavy losses they were experiencing in the Northern sectors.

Soon the day had arrived as they returned to the base camp, and the prospect of seven days leave at home. Francis now had the opportunity to return back to Sibsey Northlands, as this was his intention, but this would be soon thwarted by the Army, on the grounds of his previous desertion. Up until now he had managed to keep this from the others within his regiment, even though he had now earned a huge level of respect in his short time with the Highlanders. As the rest of the men began to leave for the seven day period, they were obviously curios as to why Francis wasn't returning home.

He accepted this, but became upset as he had to write to his mother, to tell her of this disappointment. In hindsight he should have visited whilst he was on the run with Garvin, but he knew this would have brought shame for her and the family. He now had seven days in which to do more or less whatever he liked, he considered travelling up to Calais with a view of finding Garvin, but he thought this might unsettle Garvin, and thought to let things be, until after the war. He had some back pay, so decided to travel to Paris, and to stay in a modest hotel possibly for a few days. He knew no one else in the sector, and so travelled alone using his identification card for the rail journey into Paris.

He arrived in Paris from Reims at the railway station of Garde de Nord, as his first call upon arrival inside the station concourse was the 'laver et balayer vers le haut' (wash and brush up) booth, located at the corner of the concourse. Inside were three other Soldiers, two French and one British Officer, and for one franc, his uniform and boots were all cleaned whilst he waited. The Officer asked him to what unit he belonged, and why he was in Paris, the Officer was aware of the 51st Highlanders leaving the Marne front line and taking leave, so he wrote down an address and passed this to Francis where he would find accommodation in Paris. It was a religious order of monks who resided at a monastic lodge within the city, and took in Soldiers whilst on retreat, or convalescence. He thanked the Officer, dressed himself back into his newly cleaned uniform, and then made his way out of the station. As he walked though the station entrance, the sight of the Eiffel Tower in the distance greeted him to his arrival in Paris. He asked a station porter directions to the address given by the Officer, who highlighted in broken English, the direction of four stops along the Metro, from the Garde de Nord.

The monastery seemed to be a run down place, and was located in a suburb of Paris known as St Denis. A man in civilian clothing answered the door to him and he was invited inside, as he asked for a room. The man only spoke French, as he couldn't understand as he tried to explain, soon the conversation was picked up by a member of the order, who spoke in fluent English and welcomed him to the monastic order. He was shown to a clean single room with a bed, and the only decorative item being a small wooden crucifix fixed to the wall above the bed head. In comparison to the past few weeks this was so luxurious, and had the facility to have a strip wash and shave each day. During his stay he didn't have much contact with any of the monastic order during these few days, and he was able to come and go as he pleased. He was never asked to take part in morning or evening prayers, and so was able to enjoy the sights of Paris, and to collect some pictorial postcards for his mother, and to send once he was back in camp. The Eiffel Tower, Champs Elyse, Montmartre, Notre Dame, were all visited, as he even managed both a show and cinema, although both were presented in French. He thought so much about Mary, and how he wished she could have been here to experience Paris with him. He wrote her a letter everyday that he was in Paris, with a view to posting them once he was back at camp. It was soon time for him to return back to camp, and as he was putting the last of his things together in his kitbag, a loud explosion could be heard outside, as he looked through the small window he noticed people just running about in the street, and embracing each other. Suddenly the door to his room burst open, and in ran the civilian Caretaker "soldat, soldat la guerre est finie!"as he hugged Francis tightly.

Francis was just totally oblivious of what he was trying to say, just smiled and acknowledged his joy. He repeated again "la guerre est finie, la guerre est finie."

He led Francis by the arm and outside into the street, another explosion possibly from a cannon followed as people were now actually dancing, and cheering. A man approached him, and spoke in broken English whilst vigorously shaking his hand "tommy the war est over." he just sat backward onto a garden wall, as he watched the proceedings happening in the street. This was it, he was actually going home and would now be able to serve the remainder of his court marshal , and return to some form of normality and back to work. He returned back to his unit at the camp near to Riems, and was joined two days later by the remainder of the Highlanders full of stories about their leave, and of celebrations at home, as a result of the war ending.

Over the next few days Francis considered his own future, to either return to Lincolnshire, his family, and to revert back to his role as an agricultural labourer, or to try his luck in Sheffield with Garvin, and continue as to where they had left off, before the raid at 'Sky Edge.' Sheffield also meant seeing Mary, he wanted to see her after all of this time away. His option were now clear, as he decided he would return to Lincolnshire to see his family, and then try to make his way and hopefully a future with Garvin back in Sheffield. His mind thought of nothing else but returning home, but before any decision could be made, both he and Garvin would have to serve the remainder of their court marshal before any demob. As the date arrived for the Highlanders to return home, this being before Christmas, Francis was then summoned over to the Marne headquarters, to learn of his fate. Much to his surprise he was to stay on in France, undertaking further logistical duties, until the end of January, where he would then be honourably discharged from service. Although he didn't know the fate of Garvin, it was explained to him that his Commanding Officer had presented a statement regarding his rescue of the trapped men as a result of the German bombardment of the trench. He was so relieved at this news and of him now actually going home, as the month of January seemed endless to arrive.

The day had eventually arrived, the weather was not very good for travelling but Francis didn't care, as the train slowly headed north, through the devastation and remnants of the war scarred landscapes. He travelled through Calais, and across the English

Channel to Dover, and then onward to Boston through London. From Boston he caught the Omnibus back toward Sibsey Northlands retracing the route he had taken three years earlier, but noticeably without any of the other young men who had accompanied him on that journey. The Omnibus passed through Sibsey, and slowly reached Northlands, nothing looked to have changed in the three years he had been away, as he proudly walked along Northlands Lane back toward the family cottage. Suddenly several villagers appeared at their garden gates, all wanting to shake his hand, and to welcome him home. Although he welcomed this, he didn't want to spend any time talking, and he just wanted to get to the cottage as quickly as he could. He just stood outside the cottage, no doubt so relieved that here he was, after over three years away just to see this place again. His mother immediately saw her eldest son through the kitchen window, as she ran down the garden path to meet him. She hugged him for over ten minutes, just unable to let him go.

After the greeting from his mother, William was soon reunited with the rest of his family, as his younger brothers had now both returned home from work. He had never mentioned to any of his family about his disappearance from France, that previous year. He was asked about this by his brother, as the Military Police had searched the house, following his desertion from France. As he explained to them it was a mix up with another William Francis, as he had still been over in France until two days earlier, when he was granted his honourable discharge papers.

He spent the next two weeks living at home, as he could not imagine himself retuning to life as an agricultural labourer, after he had earlier sampled life living in Sheffield. He wrote several letters to Mary, as he would daily walk to Sibsey post office, and post them. Although there was a young girl around his age who worked at the post office to whom he did quite like, and following his completed service in the Army, she did highlight to him that she was interested in him. But his intention was that he wouldn't be staying around in Sibsey Northlands for much longer. He eventually broke the news to his mother that he wanted to move to Sheffield, to try to earn a decent living, and to carve out a future for himself. She realised, he had now become such an independent individual, from that young man who had left for France those three years earlier, and it was inevitable that she couldn't stand in his way. He had been through so much, and his experience in France, although this had been brutally enforced upon him.

Chapter 8 - Sheffield or Bust.

Francis wrote to Mary to explain that he would be returning back to Sheffield on the 13th of February 1919. The day had arrived, he bid goodbye to his mother and brothers, as he caught the Lincoln bound train from Stickney railway station. At Lincoln he changed platforms to board the Sheffield bound train, as he had told Mary his train would be arriving at the Sheffield Victoria railway station, at around two o clock on that day. The Sheffield bound train made its slow journey through west Lincolnshire across the River Trent, and into Nottinghamshire, briefly calling at Gainsborough, Retford and Worksop. As the train left the rural areas around Worksop, the gradual sights of heavy industry and coal mining, began to encroach upon the railway line. This so different from the rural landscape experienced during the past sixty miles. The train now began its gradual descent into the smoky haze of the eastern side of industrial Sheffield, and the haze being much highlighted against the clear blue sky overhead on this cold February day. The train travelled through the main steel manufacturing area of the city known as Attercliffe, as Francis once more reassured to himself, that this was the right choice he had made and hopefully for him to earn some decent money, and possibly some kind of future in this 'land fit for heroes.'

The train slowed as it entered into the Sheffield Victoria railway station, the sight of the Nunnery colliery and of 'Sky Edge' could be seen perched toward the top of the valley. As the train drew to a halt, he could now see Mary sat waiting patiently for his arrival on the platform. He grabbed his case, and alighted the train as fast as he could, she ran toward him, as they both hugged for what seemed like an eternity. She passionately kissed him, and he had never experienced such closeness and affection, toward a woman before. They soon made their way out of the station concourse and along the Victoria station approach, above the very warehouse, where he had spent that first night in Sheffield, during his and Garvin's desertion during that previous spring.

In the afternoon sunlight he noticed that Mary had some bruising on her left cheek. He asked her about this, but she casually continued with the conversation about the children, and how they would both seem so grown to him now, without her even answering his earlier question. He thought nothing further of the matter as they both made their way back toward Mary's house, and along the busy Sheaf Street where they reached the Corn Exchange, and turned left along Broad Lane. He asked about Garvin, as she told him that he had arrived home in the new year, and he had been placed in the Middlewood Hospital to aid his recovery, until he had been discharged home only two weeks earlier. He had gone to Doncaster races on that day, and he wouldn't be home until later in the evening.

They arrived at the house, as she made them both hot tea, and it was only a matter of time before they were soon embraced again in the privacy of the house, as they both kissed. Mary then initiated as she turned and led Francis by the hand to the stairwell, where they both climbed up the narrow stairs and into the bedroom. She drew the curtains, as they both held on to each other and collapsed slowly onto the bed kissing so passionately. Both of the children were still at school, and with Garvin being away at the races, this moment was so precious to both of them, as to relay their feelings toward each other.

As they held each other he couldn't help himself from thinking this being the same bed, that she and Garvin shared, as they passionately kissed, and of his own feeling of guilt with this. But this felt so right to him, as he was so overcome with passion and he so wanted to be with Mary after all this time. Mary then stood at the side of the bed, and began to undo his shirt, before she removed her own clothing, and undid her long brown hair, from the hair pins that were holding it into a bun. In the half light of the bedroom, he could see that her left side and thigh were a mass of bruising. He again asked her what had happened, but she simply put her hand over his mouth, as they slowly began to make love. This was the first time for him, as Mary gently kissed and caressed him, the moment being so perfect for both of them to express their feelings toward each other.

They both collapsed onto the bed, and held onto each other for as long as they could in this precious time they had together. He again asked Mary about the bruising to her body, as she then finally admitted to him, it was Garvin's doing. She went on to add that since his return home from France, he always seemed to be in an angry rage, constantly scolding both her and the children about even the slightest of things, and often reacting with the use of his fist. She then admitted to him that she had never really loved Sam, but had used the convenience of him being on the run, to supplement her own existence as a widow with her two small children to care for. She had shared a bed with him, but he could often be brutal toward her. It was simply an arrangement, but hopefully now that the war in France had ended, she was hoping he could move out, either back to his mother's house or elsewhere within the Park district. Even though he could often be an aggressive and violent man before the war, she had noticed that even in the short period since his return home, the war had possibly affected him, and had changed him to a more aggressive and angry individual. They both dressed, continually kissing and holding onto each other with every opportunity, as they made their way back down the stairs.

The children had soon returned home from school as Mary prepared them all tea, and that William was to be their special guest. Both children were so excited at this prospect, as she watched them play games with him, and asked him question after question, about the war. Mary enjoyed this family scene so much, as this was so removed from the hostile situation of being with the bad tempered, and mostly drunk Sam Garvin, where the children would often disappear out of sight, until he was asleep or had gone out.

Mary cooked them all a meat and potato pie, as he sat reading by the gas mantle to the children. After tea, the children both retired up to bed, as Mary and William continued to embrace and kiss. At around nine thirty, Garvin had returned back to the house, he was so drunk he could barely open the back door to the house. As he entered he looked directly at Francis, and then broke into a smile, pleased to see his comrade once again. Ignoring Mary he just hugged Francis, as tears could now be seen running down his cheeks. She offered him the pie that she had saved, being kept warm on the range, to which he refused and poured both him and Francis a whisky.

They exchanged the stories, as to what had happened to each other after Garvin had been re-allocated to his duties, whilst Mary sat quietly knitting in the corner of the room. It was soon quite evident that Francis did notice Garvin's aggression, when he began to describe a certain Officer whilst they were with the Highlanders. He had become agitated, and then threw his whisky glass in a rage shattering it into the open fire of the range. Mary stood up, as she moved forward to clean up the broken glass, then he kicked out at her to move, as she bent down with the brush and pan, in an attempt sweep the broken glass from the rug. He then stood up, and shouted to Garvin "Sam no! That is well out of order," as he just turned looked over at Francis, and simply slouched back into his chair in his drunken state. He was soon fast asleep, Mary asked if Francis would help her to carry him upstairs, to which he duly obliged her. This was a surreal moment for Francis, the very same bed he and Mary had made love, only hours earlier was now being used by Garvin to sleep off his drunken state. They both returned downstairs, as they sat holding each other, once more.

"I will go and find somewhere to sleep for tonight, and will see you tomorrow" said Francis.

"But you won't find anywhere at this time, please stay here and sleep in the chair, I just feel so much better with you being here" asked Mary.

She went upstairs and came back down with a thick wool blanket for Francis. They passionately kissed goodnight, as she returned upstairs once more, and to share the bed with Garvin. The situation being surreal for Francis, as he tried to get some sleep on the chair. Thought's were racing through his mind, for most of the night as how to deal with this situation. Part of him felt disloyal toward the man who had supported and looked out for him in France, yet here was a woman that he so wanted to be with. As Mary rose the following morning, she made breakfast for Francis and the children. The children were then ushered off to school, as they left the house she once more turned to him, as they passionately kissed and hugged. Garvin still fast asleep upstairs in his drunken state. He asked Mary about events at 'Sky Edge,' but it was now common knowledge that George Mooney and his West Bar men were now running matters. Whilst Garvin had been away in France, he had worked his way back into the favour, with several of the Park men. It wasn't long before Mooney had taken back control, and had now recruited his own men from the West Bar area to assist him. She explained that Garvin felt as though many of the Park men, and especially Amos Ridal had betrayed him. As always George Wheyhill had remained loyal to Garvin, in the hope he would soon return from the war, and to take back control. Wheyhill had also expressed to

Mary, that he was concerned as to Garvin's recent welfare, and even his lack of interest, in the whole 'Sky Edge' operation. He agreed with her, that he would go to see Wheyhill at his home, and to find out what had happened in Garvin's absence.

Francis left Bard Street to walk the short distance up toward Wheyhill's home located just off South Street, Wheyhill had only just returned home that morning from working the night shift at the Nunnery colliery, and was in bed as Francis had arrived. His wife then woke him, as he came downstairs to greet Francis.

He explained to him about the recent events at 'Sky Edge.' he added " I had attended to all the business in Sam's absence, but around a week following the Military raid, Mooney had arrived with quite a mob, all up from West Bar. They had made it clear, that they wanted no trouble, and had just come to gamble, so we let them play. Within the hour it was noticeable that more Irish than was usual had now appeared at the ring. Suddenly myself, Harold and Frank were all jumped, we took quite a beating, as there must have been about fifteen of them, and they had all the takings off Frank. Most of the other Park men, just fled, and this was much to the amusement of Mooney and his cronies."

"Has there been an attempt to oust Mooney?" asked Francis

"No, such chance, Amos Ridal was the first back up there and soon the others followed, myself, Frank and Harold have no back up, so we have just kept a low profile, and are constantly being warned off by Mooney. This would have never happened with Sam being here, the Irish bastards."

"Sam has the know how, and the ruthlessness, to fuck the Irish bastards back off to West Bar, or even Ireland. Me, Frank and Harold, are no use on our own, they would just fuck us" added Wheyhill.

He could see the subject matter was so aggrieving Wheyhill and had no doubt that he felt part responsible, to this loss of control in Garvin's absence, but he had been 'stabbed in the back' by some of the other Park men, who everybody thought would remain loyal. He bid Wheyhill farewell, and decided to have a look around toward the top end of Duke Street, with the view of bumping into any of the other Park men. He went into the New Inn, and much to his surprise Sam Garvin was already sat inside, and drinking whisky, at so early in the daytime.

"Wheres tha been?" he asked Francis.

"To see George, about whats been happening up here" said Francis

"And?" he replied to him.

"Ridal, he needs fuckin sorting, lets get a message through to Mooney that were back" said Francis

"Reight, me, thee, and George, come on there's about twelve fuckin Paddies with that bastard" sarcastically replied Garvin.

"Kidnew and Keyworth? Look we gather some momentum and Mooney will then worry. It's no good rolling over, and just letting him in, he only knows one lesson."

"We start with Ridal, and move through them all one by one" Francis replied confidently.

Garvin now began to listen, as if something had switched on inside him, from that earlier gloom, as he sat upright and looked directly at Francis.

"Reight then we jump Ridal tonight, do it away from the Park, they will all be in the Durham Ox later, and the Paddies usually spend the last hour back in the Crofts. Ridal lives at Heeley, so he will usually catch the tramcar near to the Forge, and then travel up to London Road, where he usually calls in the White Lion opposite the Heeley railway station, we can jump him there" Garvin was at last showing some conviction in his outlook, which had quite surprised Francis. Maybe the presence of Francis had helped to re-kindle some of his earlier ruthlessness, and of his desire to get back at Mooney.

They both stayed for a couple more drinks in the New Inn, before they proceeded over to Harold Keyworth's house, and left a message for his wife to pass on to him. Wheyhill had to work the nightshift at the Nunnery colliery that night, but was able to supply another workmate, a man called Ronald White who had regularly attended Sky Edge, he knew Garvin quite well, and of the current circumstances of the Park men. A message was also passed on to Frank Kidnew, at his workplace in Sidney Street.

They were all to meet later that night in the Truro Tavern just off St Mary's Road. Where they would then catch the Woodseats bound tramcar from Queens Road, to the White Lion pub, and await for Ridal's return back to Heeley. They had decided to wait in the nearby Red Lion pub located about fifty yards along the road from the White Lion, and was also an ideal vantage point to see the tramcar arrive, outside of the Heeley picture palace. Directly across the road from the White Lion and built into the stone wall of Heeley station, was small gentleman's public toilet. It was agreed to carry out the assault from the inside of the toilet, and well out of view of the main London Road. It was now nine thirty when the tramcar then slowed at the stop adjacent to the Heeley picture palace, as the outline of Amos Ridal in his long overcoat and trilby hat, could clearly be seen from the large window of the Red Lion. The Park men quickly left the Red Lion, as Francis and White then approached Ridal. Garvin,

Keyworth, and Kidnew stood waiting inside the public toilet. As they neared toward the public toilet Francis suddenly punched Ridal directly into his stomach, and with him reeling from this blow, both men then dragged Ridal across London Road and into the toilet, where the onslaught began.

Francis highlighted that five on to one man was by no means a fair fight, regardless of the disloyalty shown by Ridal, so himself and White now stood outside the public toilet keeping a look out, whilst Garvin took the lead with Kidnew and Keyworth, in dealing out the vicious assault. Garvin was the first to administer the tirade of punches about Ridal's head, as he was soon knocked unconscious, having hit his head on the corner of one of the ceramic toilet urinals, as he now lay face down onto the cold tiles of the toilet floor. All three men continued to kick him about the torso, in his semi-unconscious state, as blood now slowly trickled from a head wound, and into the ceramic troft of the urinal. Harold Keyworth then produced his razor, to which he now slowly opened, as he lifted Ridal's head by his hair, he was about to slash him across the cheek, when the razor was kicked out of his hand by Garvin.

"No Harold, he may be a fuckin turncoat, but he were a Park man once, fuck him, he's had enough" said Garvin.

With the one last kick dealt directly into Ridal's side administered by Garvin. Keyworth picked up his razor, as he placed it carefully back into his jacket pocket. As the three men walked out of the toilets, as they joined Francis and White stood outside, in the cold February night air. They all walked calmly back toward the Heeley picture palace, and immediately caught a tramcar back toward the city centre, to the opposite side of the road, where Ridal had alighted, only fifteen minutes earlier.

Amos Ridal would not be found until around five thirty on the following morning, when he was discovered in the public toilet, by a man calling on his way to work for the morning shift. The man then ran to the nearby Chesterfield Road Police box, where he alerted the Police Officer in attendance, also beginning his morning shift. The Officer then attended to the scene, and assessed that Ridal was still alive. He and the man then carried Ridal who was still unconscious, to the outside of the public toilet, as they halted a city bound tramcar, whilst the two men and the tramcar conductor carried Ridal aboard. The tramcar was stopped outside the Midland Station, where a taxi was then commandeered to take Ridal directly to the Infirmary. Rival spent the following four days at the Infirmary where he was treated for his injuries, upon his discharge from the Infirmary, he refused to press any charges against any of his assailants, and simply told the Police he did not recognise any of the men that were involved in the assault.

Mooney had soon learned of the assault on Ridal, and of it being undertaken in Heeley, did not assume it to be the work of Garvin, or any of the other Park men. Ridal stayed well away from 'Sky Edge' for some time after the assault, fearful that either Garvin or any of the other Park men, would follow up matters. A chance meeting that took place between Amos Ridal and Albert Foster in the city centre, as he relayed in confidence to Foster, that Garvin had been responsible for the earlier assault. As Foster quickly went up to 'Sky Edge,' and had immediately relayed this information to Mooney.

"If he wants a fucking war, then well take it to him" replied Mooney upon hearing this news.

That night George Mooney, Albert Foster, John 'Spud' Murphy and Peter Winsey all went to Garvin's house on Bard Street, with the view to assaulting Garvin. Only Mary and the children were at home, as a brick was thrown through the downstairs parlour window. Both children were petrified, as Mary grabbed them both and ran upstairs to hide. More windows were broken as Mooney called out for Garvin to come outside and fight. The scullery door was then kicked open as the men entered the house, as Mary and the children hid in the upstairs bedroom. The men began searching the house, and they soon found Mary sat in the corner of the bedroom shaking in fear. Mooney approached Mary, and began to stroke the side of her face

"Well, well, well its Garvin's little whore, where the fuck is he?" asked Mooney.

"I don't know, just leave us" cried Mary

Albert Foster was quite uncomfortable at the whole situation, and felt that Mooney shouldn't threaten and intimidate a woman like this, and directly in front of her children who were both quite hysterical at the sight of the men entering the house. Foster placed his hand onto Mooney's shoulder, as he asked him to leave it. Mooney duly obliged but first he stood up unbuttoned his trousers, and proceeded to urinate all over the double bed, much to the amusement of Murphy and Winsey.

"A little something for Sam when he gets home" as they all left the room laughing. Garvin had been with his brother Robert, Wheyhill and Francis as they drank in the Nelson Inn at Moorhead. Garvin and Francis had returned back to Bard Street at around ten o clock. They both noticed the house was in darkness, and the door had been pulled off its hinges. They quickly went inside to find Mary sobbing in the darkness, as the children held on to her. Garvin's immediate reaction was to simply ask Mary "Mooney?" as Mary then nodded back toward him. Garvin told Francis to stay there with Mary, as he left the house to go find his brother and Wheyhill.

Mary embraced Francis, as they both reassured the children and sat with them at the foot of their bed until they both fell asleep. Francis attempted to repair the door, as he fixed the broken window panes temporary with newspaper. He hugged Mary and promised her that he wouldn't let this happen again. They both sat downstairs waiting for the arrival of Garvin, and as to what revenge had been undertaken.

Garvin, his brother Robert, and Wheyhill went to Park Hill Lane, and to the house of Albert Foster, although Foster was heavily involved with Mooney and his associates, he actually lived in the Park district. The three men broke into his house, as he was dragged from his bed, and savagely attacked with pokers. Later after admitting himself to the Infirmary, to receive treatment to his injuries from the three men, the following morning he had left Park Hill Lane, and immediately caught a train to Birmingham with his wife, and not returning to Sheffield for some time afterwards.

Mooney now realised it was only a matter of time before the Park men had actually caught up with him. Garvin was soon back to his old self and was now relishing in the outbreak of this recent violence. He had soon recruited a group of reputable hard men, who mostly hailed from the Park district, but some were also banished by Mooney, during their takeover of 'Sky Edge.' Amongst these men were William Furniss, Gilbert Marsh, Ernest Chapman, Louis Handley, Charles Price, Sandy Barlow, Robert Crook, Ernest Scott, George Wheyhill, Harold Keyworth and Robert Garvin, many later to be recognised within the annals of Sheffield folklore.

Over the following weeks Mary would secretly meet with Francis, often during the daytime taking the tramcar to the Sheffield Botanical Gardens, where they could meet in an area well away from the Park district, where they would not be recognised. It cost a penny to enter the Botanical Gardens, and so would not be frequented by many people from the Park district. It was also situated in the Eccleshall area of Sheffield toward the opposite side of the city, and being a much affluent area of many grand houses. They would walk through the gardens or if the weather was poor, would spend their precious time together in the pavilions, and exotic glasshouse. Francis had now moved into an adjacent house on Bard Street, with a neighbour of Mary's which also meant that they saw each other on a more frequent basis. As they became more involved, both were keen to spend as much time together, as was possible as Mary then asked Francis what they should have to do, to be together.

He knew this is what he also wanted, but also he had the moral dilemma to consider of what he had been through with Garvin, and as to how Garvin had looked after him much like a father figure, when bringing him over to Sheffield. He knew that Garvin didn't give Mary the attention or respect that she deserved, and he was able to offer her this. She was everything that he had ever wanted, and was his only reason for him retuning to Sheffield, so soon after the war. He was happy to be here, but just like her he wanted more, than these secret liaisons.

It was the first time in his life that he had been so close to a woman, and had felt this way, his lack of experience had meant nothing whenever they were together, and they never tired of conversation. Usually they could only meet twice a week for around two hours at a time, before having to return back to their anonymity and regular existence within the Park district. Francis was still receiving an allowance paid from Garvin, although he was not that well off, but knew that as soon as 'Sky Edge' was back in the control of the Park men, his earning would increase again. He had contemplated taking a factory job, but had decided to wait until matters were settled at 'Sky Edge.' He also contemplated eloping with Mary, but he knew that wherever they went, the wages of an agricultural labourer they would always struggle to earn decent enough money that could support a family. There were so many more opportunities available in Sheffield when compared to Lincolnshire, regardless of whatever was the outcome at up 'Sky Edge.'

Garvin's attention was totally absorbed with the re-acquisition of 'Sky Edge,' and inevitably the battle for control between the fractions that were soon to take place. The newly reformed Park Brigade, were ready to take on the Mooney's, but first Garvin wanted them weakening further, and so planned for the assault of John 'Spud' Murphy. He knew that Murphy had been involved in the break in incident at his own house, but also that Murphy was quite close to Mooney, having been raised by Mooney's mother, when Murphy's own parents died, and was always looked upon as a brother by Mooney.

Murphy worked as a baker, at a small shop on Meadow Street, near to West Bar, often gravitating up to 'Sky Edge' during the afternoons, when his work was completed for that day. He began his working day at around four o clock in the morning, so it was to be agreed by the Park men, to pay him a visit at around that early time. At around nine o clock that night, Garvin, Francis, Keyworth and Barlow all went to the Raven public house, situated toward the top of Fitzwilliam Street, where they then told the publican that they were to stay there until three thirty, to which the publican had no choice as he duly obliged and continued to serve the men. Both Francis and Garvin wanted their own revenge for the attack at Bard Street, but Garvin knew that just like the earlier Albert Foster beating, an assault on John'Spud'Murphy would seriously have an impact upon Mooney's confidence.

The bakery on Meadow Street was a typical terraced street shop, with the bakehouse located in the rear room, Sandy Barlow walked up to the shop, and he calmly knocked on the door, and highlighted he wanted to buy a loaf, Garvin and Francis then went into the rear courtyard of the shop, where the door had been left open to dispel the heat generated from the ovens. Another man was working with Murphy in the bakehouse, as he left the rear bakehouse room to answer the front door to Barlow, leaving Murphy to continue with the moulding of the loaves. Suddenly through the rear door in walked Garvin and Francis, to which a shocked Murphy, then picked up a large knife, threatening to stab both men if either came near to him. He shouted out to the other man, now in the front of the shop to "go and fetch George." But he had been apprehended by Sandy Barlow. Harold Keyworth now entered through the front door of the shop, as he then sneaked into the rear bakehouse, he could see Murphy stood confronting the others with the knife, as unbeknown to Murphy, he quietly launched a severe punch directly at Murphy's back, forcing him forward and him to drop the knife.

The other man was ordered to sit quietly inside the shop whilst he was watched over by Barlow, as Garvin, Francis and Keyworth then launched their attack into Murphy. The assault was swift and merciless, as Murphy was soon on the floor of the bakehouse, as the kick's were being quickly administered by all three men. Francis in particular was relentless at his beating of Murphy, and the thought of him being part of the gang who had earlier terrified Mary and the children. Murphy was soon on the verge of unconsciousness, as Garvin raised his arm for the men to stop. He then told Keyworth to stand on Murphy's hand, and Garvin now picking up the knife that Murphy had earlier threatened against them. He knelt onto the bakehouse floor, as he pushed the knife directly across the base of Murphy's index finger. Francis flinched at what he was about to witness, as the knife sliced cleanly through Murphy's index finger, as the severed finger now lay on the bakehouse floor as blood flowed from Murphy's hand. Murphy was by now screaming, as the other man looked on in horror, at the ruthlessness of Garvin. He then calmly picked up Murphy's severed finger, and walked into the shop, where he picked up a small loaf, inserted a small hole with his own finger, and then proceeded to insert Murphy's bloodied severed finger, into the loaf.

Smiling, he then turned toward the others, and simply said "a finger roll," much to the amusement of the other Park men. Murphy was now unconscious, as Garvin turned toward the other man at the shop and said, "when tha teks him to the Infirmary, it was a bakery accident, otherwise it'll be thee."

At that point, all four men left the shop through the front door, and back out onto the quiet of Meadow Street. It was still dark outside, as Garvin was still carrying the small loaf, as they proceeded to make their way down Hoyle Street, toward the direction of Shalesmoor.

"Sandy tek us this to Trinity Street, and put it on his front doorstep," said Garvin, passing Barlow the small loaf still containing Murphy's severed finger. Barlow duly obliged and he made his way toward George Mooney's house located on Trinity Street. The men walked back toward the city centre, and were soon joined by Barlow, who had successfully undertaken the delivery to Trinity Street. Harold Keyworth wanted to attend 'Sky Edge' that morning, and to wait for Mooney and his henchmen to arrive, but Garvin as calculating as ever, told him "wait just a couple more days Harold, before we pounce." The men now reached the Park district, and so satisfied at the result of their nights work, returning to their homes for some much need sleep. Nothing further happened over the following few days as the Park men, all kept a low profile. Mooney had surrounded himself with even more hangers on, mostly from the Irish community, whilst he nervously undertook business at 'Sky Edge.' Rumours had soon reached Garvin from other punters, that he was nervous and had appeared to be agitated over the slightest of matter's at 'Sky Edge.' He was without two of his most trusted aides in both Foster and Murphy now, and as soon as gambling had ceased for the day, the group were no where to be seen, as they hastily made their way over to the relative safety of West Bar, to conclude the days business.

Garvin wanted to highlight to Mooney a false sense of security, and that matters were now even following the assaults of Ridal, Foster and Murphy, but Garvin had called for a meeting of all the Park men to congregate in the Elephant Inn at Fitzalan Square for the following Friday morning at ten o clock. His plan would be to take the Intake bound tramcar that day, toward Manor Lane and to approach 'Sky Edge' from the opposite direction of the Park district. The men were to make their way through the Hunting Lodge grounds, and across Wybourn farm situated much further along Manor Lane. The access toward 'Sky Edge' here, was quite barren and across rough open farmland used mainly for the rearing of pigs.

Assembled at the Elephant Inn that Friday morning were Sam Garvin, William Francis, William Furniss, Gilbert Marsh, Ernest Chapman, Louis Handley, Charles Price, Sandy Barlow, Robert Crook, Ernest Scott, George Wheyhill, and Harold Keyworth. They were later all joined by Robert Garvin, who had asked for a private word with Sam, before they all embarked upon their journey toward Manor Lane.

Unbeknown to Francis, was that his recent liaisons with Mary had been uncovered by Robert Garvin, following a chance sighting by Jimmy Dyson, whilst he was undertaking his fruit and vegetable deliveries to several grand houses of the

Eccleshall area. Jimmy Dyson was the market trader to whom had helped Francis and Garvin during their return to Sheffield following their desertion in 1917. He ran a successful fruit and vegetable business from the Sheffield market, and often counted many of the wealthy families of Sheffield as his customers. He had known both Sam and Robert for several years, since they had been thrown out by their father, and he also knew of the relationship between Sam and Mary, with Mary being a regular customer at his stall in the market. He was delivering with his cart onto Brocco Bank Road, when he had spotted both Francis and Mary in quite close circumstances, near to the entrance of the Botanical Gardens.

Being a loyal friend of Sam and the humiliation of Sam in this way had unsettled him, and rather than approach him directly, he quietly spoke with Robert at the market. Robert had then taken it upon himself to wait near to the Botanical Gardens, on a day when he knew Sam would away be at a race meeting, as he observed Francis and Mary embrace outside the pavilion. He needed to tell Sam of the relationship that was taking place behind his back, and for him not to place further trust, in his so called friend of Francis.

Garvin took on board the news from Robert in a calm and collective way, quite unlike as to what Robert had expected. He told Robert to keep this information quiet from everyone, and they continued with their journey. Garvin seemed to be in good spirits, and had highlighted no animosity toward Francis on the journey toward Manor Lane. The tramcar now arrived at the bottom of Manor Lane, as the men all alighted, and began the steep walk toward the top of Manor Lane. The Hunting Lodge was situated at the top of the hill on a prominent point overlooking the whole city. Chapman and Price went ahead first, with the outcome of distracting the posted 'Pikey' at that area of the approach. Unknown to the 'Pikey,' both men had developed into a conversation with him, as they approached him. He was grabbed unsuspectedly, and his whistle immediately snatched and thrown into undergrowth. Price administered a few hits toward his face, as the youth broke free was soon running away toward the direction of Nunnery colliery, and away from 'Sky Edge.' This gave the men an opportunity to approach 'Sky Edge' undetected and as a large group in which to launch the stealth attack. Garvin led the way, and like a man 'possessed,' he was going to take back what was rightfully his on this day, as an asset that belonged solely to the Park men.

They slowly approached the gambling ring, as they could see a crowd upward of around one hundred men in the area. George Mooney or any of the other West Bar men didn't notice their approach, with some of the Park men quite apprehensive, as to what reception they were to about receive. Keyworth, Wheyhill and Scott, then ran directly into the crowd of men, hitting whoever they came into contact with, regardless if these were Mooney's henchmen, or punters. Garvin and the remainder of the men waited for their attack. This had caused some panic, and brought about a total chaos at the scene, as men tried to flee the onslaught, in all directions. Francis had then spotted both the Quinn brothers in the mayhem, as he pulled Furniss by his jacket lapel to go and assist him, with his own score to settle. Soon innocent punters were scattering and running back down the hill toward Manor Oaks Road, as the scene descended into chaos. Four large Irishmen then ran at the main group which included Garvin, with pokers and lead piping all being used as weapons in the ensuing fight, as the four were quickly overcome and beaten mercilessly, by the Park men.

Francis was slashed directly across the arm by Patrick Quinn now using a razor to protect himself, as Furniss now had John

Quinn laid on the floor, and was reigning blows toward his head. Francis couldn't get near to Patrick, as he waved the razor toward every advancing moment being made by him. Patrick Quinn was soon knocked to his feet by a rock thrown by Garvin, and hitting Patrick directly to the side of his head, this enabled Francis to now settle his score, after these past two years. Mooney and several of his close aides had run away in the mayhem, and confusion of the attack.

Sam Garvin had taken no part in any of the fighting that morning, now sat on a large rock as he watched the scene unfold before him, the scene resembled a medieval battlefield as men were now laid on the floor, in an unconscious or semi-conscious state. A number of the Irish men overcome by the Park men had continued in their attempt to get back up, and their desire to continue to fight. These men were so tough and were much admired by Garvin, in their refusal to accept they were beaten regardless of their injuries. The group of around fifteen West Bar men including Mooney, had now fled or were mercilessly dealt with by the Park men. Several were now sat on the ground, exhausted by their exertion and nursing their own injuries. It later transpired that both Gilbert Marsh and Sandy Barlow required to be taken to the Infirmary for the treatment for a broken arm, and a severe head wound, as Garvin sent Robert down to the New Inn to summon a taxi for both men.

The adrenaline of the Park men was so high that morning as they left the site, and all made their way down the hillside, toward the direction of the Durham Ox. Several of Mooney's men including both Quinn brothers were still unconscious as the Park men left the site for the Durham Ox. What was so surreal to Francis, was that here was a site that only thirty minutes earlier, was the scene of such a violent battle to control a piece of land, and was now left practically deserted as men left the site. Although no gambling would take place for the remainder of that day, it was to be expected that matters would return to normal on the following day, and this time now under the control of the Park men.

All of the Park men were then treated to drinks and food in the Durham Ox, all paid for by Garvin where they now spent the remainder of that afternoon. Garvin laughed and joked as if nothing was bothering him and showed no animosity toward Francis during that afternoon, although he had been made aware of his secret liaisons with Mary. The men were all in boisterous high spirits, which quite reminded Garvin of life back in the trenches. The men progressively getting worse for drink as the afternoon wore on. Francis was particularly pleased at being able to settle his score with the Quinn's, thanks to Furniss, as took comfort from this. Around eight o clock many of the men had either dropped off into a drink induced sleep inside the tap room, or had drunk themselves back to being sober, such were the celebratory quantities of alcohol that were being consumed that day.

No one had noticed Garvin leave the pub, as he made his way back home to Bard Street. On his return Mary had already put both children to bed, as he entered the house in his inebriated state. He then confronted Mary about her affair with Francis. She immediately denied this to him, as he now began to hit her. He grabbed her by her throat and pinning her up against the scullery wall, this woke the children who called downstairs for her, as she reassured them both she was all right, and to stay upstairs.

"How many times, you fucking bitch?" was his next question.

"And with my so called trusted friend, you fucking cheating cow."

As he slapped her across the face, then punched her so hard in the stomach that she reeled over, and was physically sick onto the floor. She managed to pull herself up the stairs to go to the children now crying and upset at the commotion that had happened downstairs. Garvin then slumped down into a chair as he began drinking from a whisky bottle. He had soon passed out into a drunken slumber, as Mary tried to reassure the children that everything was now all right.

She slept with the children in their bed that night, and with Garvin unconscious in the chair downstairs. She couldn't sleep at all, due to both the pain from her injuries, but also concluded that she now needed to get away from Garvin, now her affair with Francis had been highlighted. At first light, she and the children crept out of the house. Her first point of call would be the house to where Francis was lodging located further along Bard Street, as she told the children to wait in the side passage to the court of the house. She hammered onto the back door at the early hour. Soon the landlady of the house answered the door to her, she looked at the distressed state of Mary and quickly invited her inside. Mary had no time to wash, or to even comb her hair, such was her haste to leave her house. The lodging house had a mirror hanging onto the rear wall of the room, as she looked at her bloodied and bruised face. She flinched with pain from her torso at each time that she moved, as the landlady now went upstairs to wake Francis. As Francis appeared half dressed the landlady left them both in the room alone. Francis reeled at the sight of her in this state, as he attempted to bathe the wounds to her face.

"He knows about us, Robert spotted us at the Botanical Gardens, and has told him."

"If he hadn't been so drunk last night, I feel I would have been Hospitalised or even worse, you must go and leave Sheffield now" as she reasoned with him.

"What about you?" Francis asked her.

"I have come to ask you for some money, a train ticket for me and the children, I will have to go home to my family back in Lincolnshire."

Francis held on to her, shocked that a man could inflict so much aggression toward a woman, as he desperately wanted to go and confront Garvin for his part in all of this, but Mary wanted matters leaving. She had nothing with her except for the children, and the clothes to which she was standing in, all her valued possessions were back at the house, but she had no hesitation in her desire to abandon everything in leaving Garvin. Francis was taken aback at the next statement, as Mary asked him to come with her, and back to Lincolnshire. With no hesitation, he immediately agreed to this, as he quickly returned to his room to collect up his possessions, whilst Mary now brought the children into the house.

He realised that his relationship with Garvin could never be repaired following this news, he had helped to secure 'Sky Edge' back to the Park men, and would possibly now be due a share of the takings, but he chose to turn his back on this, and to leave with Mary.

After settling up his debt with the landlady, they all boarded the Lincoln bound train, and left Sheffield behind them, forever on that day.

On their return to Lincolnshire, Francis was offered temporary work helping on Mary's father's farm, until he managed to secure an agricultural labourer role complete with tied cottage, as part of a large farm complex at Holland Fen, near to Boston.

They were both married at Brothertoft Church on the 16 June 1921, and soon after Mary was pregnant with her third child a boy, to whom they named William after his father. Francis continued working as an agricultural labourer at Holland Fen for the remainder of his working life, and continued to live in the tied cottage, until his death in 1977. He was survived by Mary for another two years, until she passed away in 1979. They both never returned to Sheffield following their return home to Lincolnshire, they were never well off, and both managed on a typical agricultural labourers wage for the remainder of their days. They never heard anything more of Sam Garvin, or of contact from any of the Park men, following their departure from Sheffield, on that day.

In the annals of Sheffield history, both Samuel Garvin and George Mooney, later went on to become household names within the city, due to their notorious struggle for the control of 'Sky Edge,' at a time of great depression and hardship within the city during the 1920s. The seeds had already been sown, following Garvin's return from France, in the epic struggle for Sky Edge, which went on to involve many individuals with a vested interest in the money to be made at Sky Edge, and of the violence associated with the struggle. Francis never received any such share for his involvement, and he often thought of the promises that were made by Garvin during those early days, in what might have been so different in other circumstances. The violence and intimidation between both fractions eventually being brought under the control of the authorities by the mid-1920s, and the controversial Policing tactics of Chief Inspector Stiletto with the creation of the 'Flying Squad' in dealing justice to the gangs, in the only way that they understood.

'Little Chicago' was the term often used to describe the city of Sheffield during the early nineteen twenties, and William Francis would be an integral part in the creation of that reputation. Other such men benefitted from this lifestyle, of the money, and of the respect afforded to being part of the gang, but Francis was content to have turned away from this lifestyle, and all for the love of Mary.

Printed in Great Britain
by Amazon